W9-CNV-702

FREE DOWNLOAD!

Check out
Amber Road's hit song

"beautiful girl"

You can
download the song for free
and learn more about the band at:

www.myspace.com/amberroad
www.dlgarfinkle.com
www.penguin.com

Berkley JAM titles by Debra Garfinkle

the **Band**

holding on

DEBRA GARFINKLE

BERKLEY JAM, NEW YORK

A Parachute Press Book

THE BERKLEY PUBLISHING GROUP
Published by the Penguin Group
Penguin Group (USA) Inc.
375 Hudson Street, New York, New York 10014, USA
Penguin Group (Canada), 90 Eglinton Avenue East, Suite 700, Toronto, Ontario M4P 2Y3, Canada
(a division of Pearson Penguin Canada Inc.)
Penguin Books Ltd., 80 Strand, London WC2R 0RL, England
Penguin Group Ireland, 25 St. Stephen's Green, Dublin 2, Ireland (a division of Penguin Books Ltd.)
Penguin Group (Australia), 250 Camberwell Road, Camberwell, Victoria 3124, Australia
(a division of Pearson Australia Group Pty. Ltd.)
Penguin Books India Pvt. Ltd., 11 Community Centre, Panchsheel Park, New Delhi—110 017, India
Penguin Group (NZ), 67 Apollo Drive, Rosedale, North Shore 0745, Auckland, New Zealand
(a division of Pearson New Zealand Ltd.)
Penguin Books (South Africa) (Pty.) Ltd., 24 Sturdee Avenue, Rosebank, Johannesburg 2196,
South Africa

Penguin Books Ltd., Registered Offices: 80 Strand, London WC2R 0RL, England

This book is an original publication of The Berkley Publishing Group.

PRINTING HISTORY
Berkley JAM trade paperback edition / August 2007

Library of Congress Cataloging-in-Publication Data

Garfinkle, D. L. (Debra L.)
    The band : holding on / Debra Garfinkle.—Berkley Jam trade paperback ed.
        p. cm.
    Summary: The friends in the rock band Amber Road are enjoying success since they have started playing regularly at San Diego's most popular clubs, but jealousy and resentment threaten to destroy their perfect harmony.

ISBN 978-0-425-21562-3
[1. Bands (Music)—Fiction. 2. Friendship—Fiction. 3. Dating (Social customs)—Fiction. 4. San Diego (Calif.)—Fiction.] I. Title.

PZ7.G17975Bal 2007
[Fic]—dc22

2007016499

PRINTED IN THE UNITED STATES OF AMERICA

10 9 8 7 6 5 4 3 2 1

one

Tracie Grant stood with the rest of Amber Road onstage at Waves, waiting to perform. She touched the peach rose from her mother's garden she had put in her hair on a whim, bit her lip, and fiddled with her guitar strap. *Oh, God*, she thought. *Now I probably have pink lipstick all over my teeth. I hope I don't humiliate myself.* She told herself to chill, that once she started playing she'd do great, just like last week and the week before.

She was almost getting used to this. Their new manager had arranged bookings at Waves for them every Thursday night for the last month. She already knew most of the people who worked here. It was hard to believe that just a few months ago, Amber Road's biggest gigs had been at local high schools.

Tracie smiled at her best friend, Sienna Douglas, next to her on bass. They had come so far.

Mark Carrelli played scales on his keyboard to get the audience's attention. He had formed the band and managed it from the beginning. The band members still considered him Amber Road's leader. "Are you ready for us?" Mark shouted. The crowd cheered. The band was starting to attract a sizable group of fans who came to Waves just to hear them. "Three, two, one. Let's rock!" Mark yelled.

Tracie took a deep breath, planted her hands on her guitar, and started. God, it felt fantastic. The music filled her. There was nothing better than standing onstage in front of a crowd, jamming on the guitar with friends she loved. She felt that this—performing great music—was what she was meant to do. It was a rush better than the feeling of seeing another *A* grade, better than opening the acceptance letter from Yale.

Focus, focus, Tracie reminded herself. She was onstage. She needed to put her soul into the song "Don't Leave," especially since a difficult part was coming up. She moved her fingers up and down the strings, then slid close to Sienna and jammed with her.

She could tell Sienna was really into the music, moving her entire body with every strong note she played. Sienna's white cotton blouse and simple beige pants showed off her smooth, midnight black skin like a full moon lighting up a winter sky.

Beside her, Mark and his new girlfriend, Lily, were singing their hearts out, every note in synch. Lily Bouchet's singing was as fiery as she was, with her wild, reckless behavior and wavy red hair falling down her tight orange tank top to her tiny waist. Tracie couldn't help thinking that Lily was as passionate onstage as her twin brother, Aaron, was in bed.

Focus on the music, Tracie reminded herself. She could hear George Yee's tireless drums in back of her. When the bandmates were good together, they were really, really good. When they were bad, though . . .

Tonight we're good, Tracie told herself. *We had some bad times the last few months, but a lot of that was my fault. We're going to stay good. We're great. Focus on the music.*

And she did focus. On her solo, her fingers whipped across the guitar as if it were a wild, roaring beast she had just barely managed to tame. Her bandmates came in at the end for an awesome finish, and then they bowed together to huge applause.

They played more songs—the upbeat "Partytime" and "Rock It Like a Rocket," the sexy "Stray Cat" and "Touch Me, Thrill Me," and the beautiful "Love Me Like No Other." Tracie and Sienna leaned into each other as they performed. Tracie was known for her nimble fingers and creative playing. Everyone counted on Sienna on bass for her steady, perfect rhythm, always reliably right.

Their friendship was a lot like their musical gifts. Tracie usually had all kinds of drama in her life, while Sienna was more steadfast and serene. In combination, they worked well together. They had been best friends for years. Tracie smiled at Sienna as they got ready to play the last song of the night. Both of them were sweaty and out of breath. "I'm exhausted," Sienna whispered. But Tracie suspected Sienna thrived on the music and the rowdy applause as much as she did.

The last song was "Beautiful Girl," Amber Road's signature song. As loud and raucous as "Partytime" and "Rocket" were, "Beautiful Girl" was quiet and deliberate. But what the two songs shared with "Beautiful Girl" were great energy and a highly distinctive sound. Their new manager loved "Beautiful Girl" and said they should perform it whenever they could. Mark had written it especially for Lily, who joined Mark on keyboards for part of the song.

Tracie glanced at Sienna. It had to hurt Sienna to watch her ex-boyfriend so obviously in love with Lily. It was bad enough that Mark had left Sienna for another girl, but so much worse that the girl was in their band. Sienna was such a decent person, she never made a scene. *Not like all the commotion I cause when I get upset,* Tracie thought. No, Sienna was better than that. Sienna and she had both lost their boyfriends a few months ago. Sienna handled it with grace and style, while Tracie had acted like a crazy person, yelling and sobbing and almost drowning herself in the ocean.

God, she hated not having a boyfriend. She missed both her exes—Carter Branham, whom she had been with for three years, and Aaron Bouchet, whom she had stupidly left Carter for, lost her virginity with, and then ended up dating for only a few weeks. She had loved them both at different times. She supposed she still did, in a way. But she knew Aaron had never loved her back, and she wasn't sure whether Carter could ever trust her enough to love her again.

When she was dating Carter, she hadn't fully appreciated him. Now, she realized she shouldn't have broken up with Carter. It wasn't just that she hated being dateless, though she did. She thought about Sienna's fancy birthday party. It was only a week away, and she didn't have a date for it. She'd probably be a big wallflower that night, pathetically watching most everyone else coupled up. She wanted to be with Carter. But it was more than that: she missed him.

She looked for him in the audience. It was hard to see much from the stage. He hadn't been at the club before they went on. It was dumb to think he might have just showed up. Dumb, but she searched for him anyway.

And there he was! About six rows back. He was hard to miss, so tall and fair and full of energy. He must have just come in. Otherwise, she would have noticed him before. He was grinning at her and Sienna, jamming together. He would never visit a club just for fun. It wasn't his thing. So he must have come to see her. A few weeks ago, he had said he wasn't ready to get back together with her. But maybe he was now. Of course he was. Why else would he be here?

Yes! Tracie wailed on her guitar. She felt strong and sexy as she swayed her hips with the music. Hope had returned, in a major way. She watched Carter watching her. She would earn back his trust. One day soon, she would get him back. And one day, Amber Road would be the headliner at Waves instead of just playing in the middle of a four-band lineup.

Lily sang a long, high, gorgeous note to end the song. The whoops and shouts and clapping from the audience made Tracie even more determined that she could do anything. She smiled at the audience before honing in on Carter again. She thought she saw him smile back at her. Then he turned around and headed for the exit.

"Tracie!" Sienna whispered.

She looked around. She was alone onstage. God. She had been staring at Carter for so long, she hadn't noticed her bandmates leaving the stage. She followed Sienna down the steps, keeping her guitar close. She looked toward the spot where Carter had been standing, but didn't see him anymore.

"Tracie, let's go," Sienna said in front of her. "We're supposed to meet backstage."

"Coming," she said, but instead she stayed where she was, searching for Carter. But he was gone. So she headed for the greenroom, smiling as she walked. *If Carter and I get back together*, Tracie told herself, *I know I'll be happy again.*

two

What a performance! *There's nothing better,* Mark Carrelli thought, *than singing a duet with the girl you love and knocking it out of the park—or in this case, the club.* As they rushed with their instruments to the small room behind the stage, Mark felt almost as if he were flying. In the greenroom, he gently put his keyboard in its case and set it against the wall. Then he took Lily's hand and squeezed it. She squeezed it back and kissed him. Even better than performing a great song with the girl you love, was kissing her afterward.

How did I get so lucky? he asked himself. *I'm seeing a beautiful, exciting girl, my band is getting more successful every week, and now we even have our own professional manager.*

Of course, the band had been through some tough times too. Very tough. A few months ago, they had played a crazy game to switch boyfriends. The game was only supposed to last for one night, but it had repercussions far beyond that evening. After almost a year of dating Sienna, Mark left her for Lily. And Tracie had abandoned her longtime boyfriend, Carter, for Aaron, whom she had already broken up with. Mark pictured her in the ocean the night she tried to drown herself. Thank God he had found her in time. Though Mark was incredibly happy with Lily, he knew that Sienna and Tracie were still hurting.

Harry Darby popped his head into the greenroom. "Boy, oh, boy! You killed out there. Yeah, baby!" He punched the air.

Mark wanted to thank the manager of Waves, but he feared that if he opened his mouth he'd start laughing.

"Well, just wanted to let you know I'm here for you guys," Darby said. "*You* make the effort, *I* make the effort. Got to run now. Hasta la bye-bye." He pulled his head back and left the greenroom as quickly as he'd entered.

The club's bartender came in right afterward, carrying a tray full of glasses of water and soda for them. He was a big guy, not only tall but very solid. When Mark first saw him at Waves, he'd assumed he was a bouncer. "Excellent show," the bartender said. "And, Tracie, you're looking great tonight. That rose looks so pretty in your hair."

"Thanks, Brandon," Tracie said. "It's sweet of you to bring drinks over, though I was hoping you'd finally serve us real drinks. Next time, how about some Cosmopolitans or martinis?" She laughed.

Brandon shook his head, but he was smiling. "You ask me that every week. I'll be happy to serve you alcohol, Tracie," he said. "In three years, when you're legal. Hell, I'll even buy you a drink if I'm still lucky enough to know you in three years. But for now, come over to the bar anytime and I'll make you a delicious smoothie or maybe a virgin peach Daiquiri to match that pretty peach rose in your hair."

"Thanks. I did love the virgin colada you made me last week," she told Brandon before he left to return to the bar.

"What a great night," Mark said to his bandmates. "We sounded hot, Harry Darby loves us, and the crowd tonight went wild for us. Could things be any more perfect?"

"Let's celebrate. We deserve it," Lily said as she slipped her arm around Mark's waist.

He knew how he wanted to celebrate—in bed with Lily, or in his car with her, or anywhere with Lily.

"Let's do something fun," she said. "You guys want to party in this great hot tub I know about near San Diego State?"

"What's so great about it?" Sienna asked. "I have a hot tub at home. So do most of us."

"Yeah, but we also have parents at home." Lily rolled her eyes. "Who wants to sit in a Jacuzzi while your parents are staring out the window spying on you?"

Parents were not Lily's thing. Mark hadn't even ever met her parents. Mark pictured Lily sitting next to him in a Jacuzzi, or better yet on his lap in a Jacuzzi, the bubbles dancing on her lithe body. He couldn't wait. "Let's go for it," he said.

"We don't have bathing suits," Tracie pointed out.

"You're wearing a bra and underwear, aren't you?" Lily asked.

George punched his fist into the air. "I'm totally up for that."

"I bet you are," Tracie said. "I bet most guys would be up for that. Carter sure wouldn't mind, I bet." Tracie smiled when she said his name.

Mark had spotted him in the audience tonight. Was Tracie seeing him again?

"What about towels?" Sienna asked.

"We don't need them," Lily said. "Live a little. Let's go."

"I can't wait." Mark put his arm around her. One thing that made him crazy about her was that she was open to just about anything.

As they walked to the car, Lily took out her cell phone. "Just need to call my parents and make up some excuse why I'll be home late," she told Mark. Then she said into the phone, "Hi, Aaron." After a pause, she said, "They won't be back 'til Wednesday?"

Man, their parents were never home. Lily and Aaron practically lived by themselves. At first, Mark had thought it was cool. But now he suspected that Lily must feel deserted.

"At least I don't have to lie about where I'll be tonight," Lily said into the phone. "I'm going out with the band to that Jacuzzi near San Diego State. Hey, if you want to—"

"No!" Mark whispered to Lily.

"Aaron, I have to get off the phone. I hope you have a good night, okay?" She hung up. Then she turned to Mark.

"I wasn't thinking. I totally forgot that Tracie would be there."

He lowered his voice. "It would be a disaster if Tracie and Aaron were at the Jacuzzi together. You know how she fell apart after they broke up."

"I know. Sorry," Lily said. "I was just trying to be nice to my brother. I think he's all alone in the house tonight. I feel bad for him."

Mark didn't. Aaron was such an ass. But he wasn't about to say that to Aaron's twin sister. "Well, maybe he'll have people over now that your parents are gone," he told Lily.

"It's just that Aaron's been complaining that he hardly ever sees me anymore because I'm so busy with you and the band."

"I didn't know that," Mark said.

"We used to spend a lot more time together. For most of our lives, we've had to, like, totally rely upon each other. With our parents traveling so much, and moving us to different cities and countries all the time, Aaron and I have always been really close." Her voice cracked as she talked. Mark knew it was hard for Lily to lose her tough-girl act. He was glad she did. "Aaron's been, like, the only person who's always been there for me," she said.

Mark drew her close. "Lily, I'll always be here for you."

She kissed his cheek. "You're so sweet. I just have to think about Aaron's feelings too."

Mark nodded. "I get it. You're kind of in an awkward spot."

"You know what spot I'd really like to be in?" Now she was using that sultry tone that drove Mark crazy.

"What spot?"

"In the Jacuzzi right now, next to you, staring at your wet boxers."

They kissed again. Mark's thoughts about the band and Aaron and everything else vanished as his fingers ran through Lily's long, thick red hair and his tongue toured her hot, eager mouth.

three

Sienna walked out of Waves with Tracie. Not far from the door, she saw Lily and Mark standing with their arms around each other, clamped in a kiss. Sienna looked away quickly and headed for her car. She tried to be tolerant of Mark and Lily's relationship—they were her bandmates, after all—but she had her limits. And a close-up view of her ex-boyfriend making out with his new girlfriend was beyond those limits.

"We were burning up the stage, huh?" Tracie interrupted her thoughts.

Sienna was grateful for the interruption. "Yeah, we were. We were red-hot. Tracie, you were totally on fire during your guitar solos, especially toward the end of our set. It was awesome."

"Thanks," Tracie said. "Carter got me all hot."

"Carter?" Sienna hadn't meant to sound so shocked, but Tracie had told her that he had no interest in getting back together with her.

"Didn't you see him in the audience? He was smiling right at me," Tracie said. "He sure picked up my spirits."

"He was? He did?" Sienna hadn't noticed him. Why did Tracie sound so happy about him being there, anyway?

"Don't sound so shocked," Tracie said.

"Sorry." Sienna was disappointed she hadn't known he was at the club. She and Carter had become closer friends, comforting each other after they both lost their relationships the night of the boyfriend trade. They also had AP English class together with the world's most boring teacher, which meant they spent a lot of time performing exaggerated yawns during class and complaining afterward. Carter was a really nice guy, and very smart and handsome too. If he hadn't gone out with her best friend for most of high school, she might have been interested in him herself.

Tracie touched the rose in her hair. "Carter was at Waves tonight, staring at me with his little smile. I guess he's telling me he might be ready for romance again."

"You think so?" Sienna tried to fish out her keychain from her purse, but it took a while. She was so confused. Less than a month ago Tracie had told her that Carter never wanted to go out with her again. And Tracie hadn't seemed as if she wanted to get back together with him.

Tracie bounced a bit as she waited for Sienna to unlock the car door. "You don't go to a club where your ex-girlfriend is playing if you're not interested in her," Tracie said.

"But you said he was over you." Sienna tried to puzzle it out.

"Sienna, please. Can't a guy change his mind about a girl? We did date for most of high school." As they got in the car, Tracie said, "I can't believe I ever broke up with him for Aaron. I'm such an idiot."

Sienna reached over and gave her a hug. "I know you've been having a hard time."

Tracie hugged her back. "I'm so lucky to have you for a best friend. We're going to have a great time in the Jacuzzi. I could totally use some stress-free fun."

Sienna started the car and took off.

"The last few weeks have been so awful," Tracie said. "Aaron broke my heart, but being alone is almost worse."

Just hearing the jerk's name made Sienna cringe. "Nothing could be worse than the way Aaron Bouchet treated you," she told her friend. "He's a player. Next time you're bummed about being alone, remember the time Aaron brought Whitney Lowell to our club performance and freak-danced with her right in front of you."

"I know." Tracie sighed. "Aaron is a jerk. But Carter was always sweet to me. The whole three years we dated, he was a good guy. I got totally jazzed when I spotted him in the audience tonight. I really miss him, just being with him. God, Sienna, I was an idiot not to see what a great boyfriend I had at the time." She sniffed in, as if holding back tears. "Now I hope it's not too late."

"It's not," Sienna tried to reassure Tracie. "But are you sure you really want Carter back? Maybe it's just that you're not used to being without a boyfriend."

"Why should I get used to it?" Tracie said. "I hate it."

"I just don't want to see Carter get hurt again." Sienna took her hand off the steering wheel and put it on Tracie's shoulder. "That night you traded him for Aaron, he was so upset. The whole time we were driving around together, going to different sucky places, all he could talk about was you."

"I really messed up," Tracie said. "That's all I've been thinking about lately, that I messed up by breaking up with Carter. I just hope he'll take me back."

Sienna shook Tracie's shoulder playfully before returning her hand to the steering wheel. "We just need to take it slowly, that's all."

"We?"

"I'll help you get him back," Sienna promised. "I want to see you happy again."

"Thanks." Tracie smiled, but her eyes were wet.

"You guys need to go on a date, and he'll remember how good you were together." She said that as confidently as she could, though she wasn't sure she fully believed it.

"Oh, Sienna." Tracie put her head on Sienna's shoulder. "He came to the club tonight, but it's not like he asked me out. He wouldn't even stay long enough at Waves tonight to talk to me."

"We'll set up a stealth date then," Sienna said. "You guys always were so good together. I'll make it my project to help get Carter back for you."

"I'm so grateful you're my friend." Tracie lifted her head.

"How about this for a stealth date? I'll call Carter and invite him to the hot tub tonight," Sienna said. As she dug her phone out of her purse, she wished for a moment that it was *her* ex they were scheming to get back. But it was always about Tracie, and it seemed to Sienna that she was always the one who had to be strong.

"I hope Carter can come out with us tonight," Tracie said. "Thanks so much for asking him. You're such a good friend."

Sienna called Carter.

four

By the time Tracie and Sienna arrived at the address of the apartment complex in Del Cerro that Lily had given them for the hot tub, the rest of the band was already there, waiting outside the metal fence. They could see the hot tub in a courtyard near the pink stucco building. George had brought a pretty brunette girl with him. "This is Kaitlin," he said. Then he gestured toward Tracie. "And this is my friend and fellow bandmate—"

"Stacy," the girl said. "I've heard so much about you. Nice to meet you, Stacy."

"Um, actually it's Tracie. Nice to meet you too." Tracie scanned the cars rushing down the street. Carter was going to meet them here. He'd probably take a few minutes longer to arrive, since they'd just invited him, but Tracie kept an eye out for his white Prius just in case.

"Oh, good. We're all here now," Mark said as he leaned against the fence. "Let's get—"

"Towels?" Kaitlin said. "I would have brought some if you'd asked."

"Actually, I was going to say *let's get wet*," Mark told her.

"Ohh," Kaitlin said. "Why didn't you say so?"

George put his arm around Kaitlin. "You're so cute."

"You up for a little adventure, Lily?" Mark asked.

"Me?" Lily laughed. "Up for an adventure? Is the pope—"

"An anachronism? Yes," Kaitlin said.

"I was going to say, Is the pope Catholic?" Lily said. "Let's go in the hot tub already."

Why did George always bring such irritating dates? Tracie thought. She looked for Carter's car again, but still didn't see it.

"Lily, who do you know who lives here?" Sienna asked.

"I have no idea. It seems pretty empty," Lily said. "Aaron and I were bored one night a few months ago when we first moved to San Diego, so we drove around, stopped here, and climbed the fence. There were no people anywhere near the hot tub. I've been back a few times since, and it's always been deserted at night. I think mostly old folks live here. They're probably all in bed by now."

"Ooh, we're going to sneak in!" Tracie said. "Fun!"

"You want us to trespass?" Sienna asked.

"Let's live a little," Tracie told her friend. "It's our last year of high school."

"Living a little shouldn't mean getting arrested," Sienna said. "If we get caught, we're screwed."

Lily shook her head. "You're totally overreacting."

"Call it whatever you want," Sienna said. "I'm not sneaking in here. Didn't you see that sign?" She pointed to the sign on the fence just a few feet away, which read NO TRESPASSING. VIOLATORS WILL BE PROSECUTED. "The last thing I need is to get caught in a wet bra and panties and arrested for trespassing. Tracie, let's go."

"I want to stay," Tracie said. "I haven't done anything fun like this since . . ." Her voice trailed off. She was going to say *since Aaron.*

"Well, I'm going in," Lily said. She put her foot in an opening in the chain link, clutched the middle of the fence with her hands, and started climbing. Once she got to the top, she jumped down. Mark, George, and Kaitlin followed her, laughing as they fell to the ground, one by one. "You guys coming?" Lily asked Tracie and Sienna through the fence.

"Not me," Sienna said.

Tracie was dying to follow Lily. It wasn't only that she needed some fun in her life. It was also that Carter was going to meet them here any minute now. She couldn't wait to sit next to him, half-naked, in the hot, bubbly Jacuzzi water.

"I'm sorry for being a spoilsport," Sienna said. "I just don't think it's a good idea. If I got caught, my parents would freak and it would screw up my chances for that scholarship I applied for."

"It's cool," Tracie said.

Carter finally arrived. Tracie watched as he carefully parked his car and walked toward them. Even in the dusky, artificial light of the apartment complex, he looked cute with his ocean-blue eyes framed by thick blond hair. He was fair and tall and thin, like her. *We belong together,* Tracie thought.

"Hey, Carter! I'm so glad you came!" she called out. "It's going to be a blast!"

Carter folded his arms over his chest. "You mean we're supposed to sneak in here? You didn't tell me that." He pointed to the NO TRESPASSING sign on the fence. "I'm sorry, but I really don't want to get in trouble. What if we got arrested or something?"

"Come on!" Lily called from the other side of the fence. "Tracie, I thought you were all excited about doing this."

"Go ahead, Tracie, it's all right," Carter said.

"But, I—"

"I don't want to be a spoilsport," he said, using the same word Sienna had used before he got here.

"It's okay," Tracie told Carter. "I'll stay here and we can do something else."

"No. Join the group," he said. "I want you to have fun."

She knew he was just being nice. But he didn't realize the hot tub would be fun for her only if he was in it. "Sienna, you can still change your mind," she pleaded, hoping Carter would come too when he saw everyone else doing it.

Sienna shook her head. "I just can't take the risk right now of getting caught."

"Come on!" Kaitlin grabbed Tracie's hand through the chain link and pulled her toward the fence.

"Go ahead, Tracie," Carter urged. "I'll celebrate with you guys another time."

Tracie felt as if she had no choice but to follow the others. As she climbed the fence, she experienced a rush. It was almost like being with Aaron—a little crazy and dangerous and thrilling. One thing she'd learned about herself when she'd dated Aaron: she had a wild streak, which she enjoyed indulging.

As soon as her feet touched down on the other side, she asked Sienna and Carter again if they wanted to go to the Jacuzzi.

"No. Sorry." Sienna looked as unhappy and uncomfortable as Tracie felt. Obviously, neither of them had expected the night would turn out like this.

"Have fun. See you later." Carter waved to Tracie, almost jauntily. He didn't seem disappointed. "I'll walk you to your car, Sienna," Carter said. He turned around and headed to the curb, and Sienna followed him.

Perfect, Tracie thought as she headed over to the Jacuzzi. *Now that Sienna and Carter left, I'm stuck here as a third wheel with Lily and Mark. Could the night get any worse?*

George shouted, "Let's get—"

"A disease?" Kaitlin asked.

"I was about to say *Let's get going*," George said.

Yes, there were worse things than being a third wheel. For instance, being a fifth wheel, especially when one of the wheels was totally annoying. George had dated a lot of strange girls, but never one this irritating. Tracie would have her choice of watching Lily and Mark make out in the Jacuzzi, or George make goo-goo eyes at Kaitlin while she interrupted everyone.

But it was too late to catch up to Sienna and Carter. She heard a car start. They were probably driving off. So Tracie sighed and slowly followed the two couples as they made their way to the Jacuzzi.

five

"I hope those guys don't get in trouble for sneaking into the pool area," Carter said to Sienna as they walked away from the apartment complex.

"You think we were right to leave?" she asked. "The others probably think we're big prigs."

"I don't care much what they think," Carter said. "Anyway, being here with you is really nice."

She stumbled for a moment. What was that about? Was Carter flirting with her? No way. He must mean he valued her friendship.

"Do you realize we've hardly ever been alone together?" Carter asked her.

Sienna felt the best response was no response, so she headed toward her Miata in silence. Carter walked right next to her, their footsteps in perfect synch. He smelled good, like cloves and cinnamon.

"Well, sorry it didn't work out," she said as she neared her car.

"It could work out," he said. "Let's go somewhere tonight. It's still early. We could go over to my house. I have a Jacuzzi I don't have to break the law to use."

She and Carter alone in a Jacuzzi? She knew they were just friends, but it didn't feel right. She shook her head. "I wasn't that into sitting in a hot tub, anyway. How about going to Juice Caboose? We could take separate cars and meet there, right?"

"And waste gas and ruin the environment? You're asking someone who drives a Prius. Don't make me feel horribly guilty."

Sienna punched him playfully.

"I'll drive, okay?"

She shrugged. "Sure. You'll just have to bring me back here afterward to get my car."

It was a nice drive. Not because of the scenery or the roads, especially, but because of the company. She had always found Carter funny and easy to talk to. They were both in the AP-class crowd, so they had a lot in common. Sienna had hung with him before if Tracie or a bunch of their classmates was around, but he was right—they had hardly ever been alone. She discovered she very much liked being alone with him.

They pulled up to Juice Caboose, ordered the natural juices it was famous for, and kept talking. "Is that liquefied grain as awful as it sounds?" Carter asked her as they shared a tiny round table.

"Hey. Don't insult the merchandise." She put her foot lightly on his, then reprimanded herself for what could be interpreted as flirting and moved her foot away. "Just because I ordered a wheatgrass concoction doesn't mean it tastes awful," she said.

"But I bet it does, anyway." He stirred his orange smoothie with his straw. "I can tell you want to make a face and spit it out."

"Okay, maybe a little." She laughed.

"But it's got to be better than watching Lily attack Mark in the Jacuzzi or an old person cane us to death for trespassing," Carter said.

Sienna nodded. "And you should have heard George's date. I was ready to cane her to death myself."

"You could have tortured her first by making her drink wheatgrass," Carter said.

Sienna laughed again. Damn, Carter was funny. Mark was so serious all the time. Not that Carter wasn't every bit as driven as Mark—a person had to have serious goals to get into Yale—but he talked about silly things too.

She stopped laughing. She shouldn't compare Mark and Carter. Mark was her ex-boyfriend. Carter was just her friend.

Carter leaned forward, and she breathed in the sweet cinnamon-clove aroma of him again. "It's great talking to you by yourself for a change." He smiled at her. He had a charming dimple on one cheek. Had she ever noticed that before?

She could understand why Tracie wanted him back. She told Carter, "Tracie was really happy about you coming to Waves tonight."

"I'm glad Tracie's happy," Carter said. "She's doing okay now. Good for her."

"I think she misses you, a lot," Sienna said.

"It's a tough adjustment," Carter said. "We went out for so long. How about you? You getting over Mark?"

No one had really asked her that before. Tracie didn't need to, Sienna supposed. They told each other everything, so she didn't have to ask. Still, it seemed like they spent a lot more time talking about Tracie getting over Carter and Aaron than they did on Sienna's feelings about Mark.

"Sienna? You look bummed all of a sudden," Carter said. "You thinking about Mark?"

She shook her head. "Actually, no. It was really hard for me at first, seeing Mark with Lily. I hated them both for being together. I wanted him back so badly."

Carter's brows furrowed.

"But now, I think things are different," she said. "Mark and Lily seem so happy together, like they absolutely belong with each other. I bet you've noticed the way he looks at her, like he's amazed by her, amazed at his fantastic fortune of being with her. He doesn't say it out loud, but it's obvious." She chewed on her fingernail. "Mark and I never had that, really. I mean, we loved each other. I know I loved him. But I don't think either of us ever thought we'd found the one person we were destined to be with forever."

Carter nodded. Sienna wondered if he had felt destined to be with Tracie forever. "You and Mark seemed happy together," Carter said.

"We were. But after we broke up, I realized he wasn't . . . Oh, this sounds corny."

"Tell me." Carter leaned toward her.

He smelled so nice. Tonight Sienna felt as if she could tell Carter everything she'd kept inside for so long. *That's good,* she told herself. *Friends can talk to each other honestly.* She cleared her throat. "I realized Mark wasn't my soul mate, my one true love. And I wasn't his either," she said.

Carter didn't laugh or roll his eyes like she'd feared. Instead, he asked, "What made you realize that?"

She sighed. "It wasn't one thing. It was a lot of things, built up. For example, he used to give me flowers for Valentine's Day, and chocolate and stuff on my birthday. But now I think he did it because it was what he was expected to do. I hope there's a guy out there for me who does more than that. I want someone who thinks about me on a day that's not a holiday or whatever, and gives me candy just because he loves me. And maybe I would bake him a cake or something for no reason except that I want to do something sweet for my one true love." She sighed. "Jeez, you must think I'm crazy, huh? Or spoiled or something."

"Not at all, Sienna," Carter murmured, his voice like velvet. "In fact, I think you deserve flowers for no reason."

Sienna looked away. Was he flirting with her? *No,* she decided. *He's just being a sweetheart.* She had to help Tracie get him back, and she wasn't helping at all by pouring her heart out to him. Sienna stood up. "We'd better go. You said you'd drive me to my car."

He stood up too. "Of course."

She hurried out the door.

six

Tracie walked to the Jacuzzi, trailing the others. "Last one in's a rotten egg," Lily said. "Get your clothes off."

Mark laughed. "Let me help you, Lily." They went off together in the dark, giggling and throwing their clothes on the ground, and God only knew what else.

Tracie moved to the darkest corner of the Jacuzzi area and turned her back on the group. She was happy for Mark and Lily, but their closeness made her feel lonelier than ever. Maybe Carter would change his mind and head to the hot tub after all. Seeing everyone else coupled up might put him in a loving mood again. She listened for him, but heard only splashing sounds.

George called out, "The Jacuzzi's great! You coming in, Tracie?"

She reluctantly undressed down to her underwear and joined the others in the warm water.

"I told you no one would be here," Lily said.

"In that case . . ." George reached behind him and took a bottle out of a bag. "Corona, anyone?"

"Dude!" Lily said. "Awesome."

"Ladies first." George handed bottles of beer to Lily, Kaitlin, and Tracie. "It's party time!"

Tracie listened for Carter again. He didn't drink, and probably wouldn't like to find her with a beer in her hand. She didn't hear anyone coming. *Screw it,* she told herself. *I could use a beer.*

So she took a big swig. It felt so good after all the stress of the last few months. Carter had made things even worse tonight, acting as if he couldn't care less about leaving the apartment complex without her.

She chugged down the rest of the beer. Everyone was drinking, joking around, splashing each other, having a good time. *I don't need Carter,* she told herself as she laughed at George's imitation of their new band manager, Steve Guyda, barking and growling like a bulldog.

"We can laugh all we want," Mark said, "but Steve Guyda's the best thing that's ever happened to Amber Road."

Tracie opened another bottle of Corona. "A drink in honor of our new manager!" she said.

"To Guyda making us rock stars!" George drank some of his beer.

Tracie happily took another swig. They really could become rock stars. Not only was Guyda getting them booked at clubs, but on Monday he was meeting them at a studio so they could record their best songs. Soon she'd be too busy with her music career to give Carter a second thought. She didn't need him.

Then Mark and Lily started making out, and soon George and Kaitlin followed their lead. Tracie started on another Corona. She *did* need Carter. If only he were here, she wouldn't feel so bored and alone. *How could he have left me?* she thought as she drained the bottle. When she had climbed the fence earlier, she hadn't expected to spend most of the evening essentially by herself, listening to the sounds of kisses and heavy breathing.

As she drank, she tried to think how she could win Carter back. She would have to take it slow, think up an excuse to get together with him rather than just asking him outright. Sienna said she'd help. She'd need to run into him "accidentally," or come up with a good reason why she and Carter needed to be alone together.

She heard footsteps rushing toward them. Carter? No. He was always so deliberate. He never rushed anywhere. Was it a security guard from the apartment complex?

Oh, God. That was all she needed, to get caught almost naked, trespassing and drinking! And she wasn't even having a good time. Sienna and Carter would say *I told you so,* or at least they would think it. "Someone's coming," Tracie whispered loudly. "Maybe we should jump out of the water and run to the gate."

Mark and Lily finally took a break from their kissing marathon. "Wait," Lily said. "The person might leave. Or maybe he won't exactly mind having half-naked teenage girls with him in the water."

"I think we should go," Tracie urged. She didn't want to be here, anyway. Not without Sienna and Carter.

The man came closer. In the dim lighting of the Jacuzzi area, Tracie could just make him out. "Oh, God," she said. It was Aaron.

"Lily," Mark whispered. "I thought you weren't going to invite your brother. Why didn't you at least warn us that Aaron was meeting us here?"

"Jeez, Mark. I had no idea," Lily said. "I mean, I called and said I'd be out late because I was coming over here. You heard me on the phone with him. But he never said he was planning to join us."

As Aaron approached and took off his tight T-shirt, Tracie sucked on the top of her beer bottle. *Don't let him get to you,* she told herself. *He may have a great body and he can turn on the charm, but you know what a jerk he is.*

He sat on the cement behind her. "Tracie, I was hoping you'd be here." He took off his shorts and flip-flops, then lowered his voice to a whisper. "Even though we're not a couple anymore, you'll always be my gorgeous girl."

Gorgeous girl. Aaron was the only person who ever called her that. *Those are just words,* she told herself. *Empty words.* She wanted to slap him. She wanted to tell him off. She wanted to kiss him. She wanted most of all to have never met him before.

He squeezed in next to her in the Jacuzzi. She told herself to be brave, remembered that he'd fooled around on her practically the entire time they'd been dating. She slid a few inches away from him.

"I know you don't ever want to be with me again," he said. "So don't worry. I won't try anything tonight."

"You better not." Tracie crossed her arms. But, God, she liked seeing his broad chest up close.

Aaron pointed to Kaitlin, who looked like she was sitting with one leg over George's. "Your date, George, I presume?" he asked.

"Hey, Aaron," George said. "This is Kaitlin."

Aaron grinned, "Nice to—"

"Have a Jacuzzi available. I know. Even if we have to hop a fence to do it," Kaitlin said.

"I was going to say *Nice to meet you*, but that's okay," Aaron said.

The other couples returned to make-out mode, with giggles and happy sighs. Tracie couldn't help remembering when she and Aaron had made out, made love. It used to be so good.

"We were good together, Tracie," Aaron murmured as if he knew just what she was thinking.

We were good together when you weren't cheating on me and breaking my heart, Tracie thought but didn't say. She'd already broken up with him and told him why. Tonight, drinking Coronas in the Jacuzzi among her friends, wasn't the right time to tell him off again. Besides, he had said he wouldn't try anything, and she was glad to have company apart from the kissing couples.

So they sat for a while with a little space between them and chatted about school and the band and made dumb small talk. Maybe it was the beer or maybe it was Aaron's promise to be a gentleman, but she actually had an easy time making conversation with him. They even laughed together.

At one point, he whispered, "I miss you, gorgeous." She told him not to talk like that and he apologized, but really she liked hearing it. What girl wouldn't want to be called gorgeous? And *Carter* certainly hadn't complimented her tonight. Carter had barely acknowledged her.

Tracie was starting on another beer and feeling like a prune in the water when Mark said, "Hey, Lily and I are going to take off. We'll drive you home, Tracie." He smiled as he talked. Lily was sucking on his neck. "Okay?" he asked.

"Well, that sounds like fun," Aaron said drolly. "A romantic car ride with just the three of you."

"I can drive you—" George started to say.

"Crazy. I know you can drive me crazy. Yowza!" Kaitlyn exclaimed and threw her arms around George.

"I'll take you home, Tracie," Aaron offered.

She shook her head.

"Don't worry, gorgeous. I'll be a complete gentleman," he said. "And Mark, I know you have a thing about drinking and driving. Out of respect for that, I only had one beer."

"Tracie, I can drive you. Really," Mark said as Lily licked his ear.

"It's all right." She had witnessed more than enough of their make-out sessions in the hot tub tonight. The last thing she needed was a car ride filled with more sucking noises and whispers and giggles. "I'll just go home with Aaron," Tracie said. She looked into his dark, long-lashed eyes. "Can I trust you?"

"Of course," Aaron said.

She held up her Corona. "Anyone want this? I only took one sip."

"Keep it." Aaron pushed the bottle toward her chest. "One for the road, right?" He put his hand on her thigh.

She took it off. "Wrong. I've had too many of these already. And you'll be a perfect gentleman?"

"I promise. I'll even close my eyes while you get out of the water and put your clothes back on."

So she left the hot tub and got dressed. But when she glanced over her shoulder as she put on her shirt, she noticed he was gawking at her. "Aaron!"

"Sorry." He winked at her. "I try to be a gentleman. But when it comes to you, sometimes I just can't resist."

He'd better resist, Tracie thought. *And I'd better resist too.*

seven

Tracie sat in Aaron's Porsche and leaned against the door. She felt happy, tired, woozy. She hadn't drunk so much in a long time. It wasn't as if she'd been laying off alcohol though. About a month ago, she'd found close to a full case of beer in her garage, left over from her mother's fortieth birthday party almost a year earlier. Her parents hardly ever drank. She knew they wouldn't notice if she took some beer. She had a bottle in her bedroom a few weeks ago, after coming off two hard midterms. Then she drank another beer a few nights later when she couldn't stop thinking about Carter and Aaron. Drinking alone wasn't the same as drinking with a boyfriend, but that didn't stop her from having another beer that same night. Soon her two bottles of beer had become a nightly ritual and the case was almost gone. She didn't know what she'd do when her parents noticed the missing beer. Maybe they'd blame it on the gardener or the housecleaner, or her sister, who recently had visited from UC Santa Cruz. She also didn't know what would happen when the case of beer ran out. "Whoa!" she said as the car bounced through a pothole. She giggled.

"You okay?" Aaron asked.

"Mmm," Tracie answered. "Thanks for the . . ." She hoped her parents wouldn't notice how drunk she was. Because she'd been a goody-goody all these years and gotten into Yale, her parents trusted her. She didn't want to ruin that trust. She would just tell them she was really tired and head straight—or crookedly—for her room. She didn't think she could walk straight tonight.

"Thanks for the what?" Aaron asked.

God, she was so wasted she'd forgotten whatever it was she'd been talking about.

He put his hand on her thigh. "Thanks for the amazing sex we used to have?"

"Aaron. That's over."

"You were always so hot. You loved it." He moved his hand up.

"Aaron, please," she said.

"Please what?" His hand stayed where it was. "You're just so sexy. You want to know how much I missed you?"

"No. Don't tell me, Aaron." Because if he did, if he started going on about how gorgeous she was, with his hand caressing the inside of her thigh, and her not able to think straight anyway after all those beers, she wasn't sure she could keep resisting him. The thing was, she had missed him too. Oh, she had been mad at him, and he had made her cry, and she knew he couldn't be trusted. But she missed sitting on Aaron's lap, wrapped in his muscular arms. She missed his kiss, his touch, making love, and lying next to him afterward, listening to his steady breaths as he slept. She sighed.

"Okay. I won't tell you how much I miss you. I won't say that I think about you every night, about how gorgeous you are, about your soft voice and your long neck and your pretty hair."

"Oh, Aaron." Her voice was breathy and weak. She leaned into him. God, it felt so good to feel a guy's touch again.

"Can't I pull over and kiss you, Tracie? For old time's sake. We don't have to do anything else. Just kiss." He returned his hand to the steering wheel.

"Okay, just kiss. Then you'll drive me home. You promised to be a . . ." What was the word? God, she was so wasted. "A gentleman."

Aaron pulled into a turnout and stopped the car. Somehow they'd gotten on a mountain road. She hadn't even noticed.

"Hey, this isn't on the way to my—" Before she could say *house*, Aaron took off his seat belt and grabbed the back of her head and kissed her.

It wasn't as good as she'd remembered it. For one thing, she felt slightly nauseated from all that beer. And kissing him now, now that she knew what a jerk he was, wasn't the same as kissing him when she thought she loved him. But she kissed him back, mostly because she'd already told him she would.

Then his hand went to her chest. She pulled away from him and said, "No. Just kissing. That's it."

"Please, Tracie, I want you real bad." He climbed over the stick shift to her. "We were so good together," Aaron said.

They *were* good together, and it did feel good now. She told herself, *It's just for fun and no one will know.* So they made out for a while in his Porsche on the side of the mountain. He knew just where to touch her. How could something that felt so good be bad?

"Come on, Tracie. It feels so good," he whispered.

"No!" she said. She was drunk, but she knew this was wrong. She thought she did, anyway. She shouldn't have even fooled around with him, but at least she could muster up sense enough not to have sex with him. "Take me home," she said.

"But, Tracie." He put his hand on her thigh again.

"No." It wasn't like old times at all. In old times, she had believed him when he called her gorgeous. Now she didn't feel gorgeous at all. Tonight, she felt ugly. "You promised to be a gentleman. Remember? Stop." She pushed his hand away.

He grimaced. "Okay, but you're really missing out."

"Mmm, I guess so," she murmured. "You're right. I'm really . . ." Really what? She was so tired. What was she going to say? She leaned her head against the car door to think about it, and fell asleep.

As she dozed off, she thought she saw flashing lights and heard clicking noises, but she kept her eyes shut, as if nothing bad could happen if she didn't see it.

She must have passed out, because the next thing she knew Aaron was shaking her and telling her that they were at her house. She stumbled up her driveway, leaning on him the whole way. At her front door, he said something about it being a memorable night.

"My keys," Tracie said, putting what little energy she had into trying to get inside her house.

"You can't even find your house keys you're so wasted." Aaron laughed. "You know you're gorgeous even when you're passed out cold." After fumbling in her purse, Aaron pulled out Tracie's house keys. "Aren't you going to thank me for the ride?" he asked.

So she mumbled, "Thank you," as he opened the front door for her and helped her in.

She made her way through the dark house to her bedroom, desperately hoping she—and Aaron—would forget what had gone on tonight.

eight

The next day, Tracie and Sienna left AP History together and headed toward the cafeteria. Tracie walked with her head down. She hadn't seen Aaron at school today, but that wasn't surprising. She had mostly AP classes, while he didn't even take any honors courses. It was lunchtime she was dreading. Aaron usually sat near the entrance to the lunch area, where everyone passed by. He would wave and call out to people he liked, ignore the others. She suspected he'd call out to her, maybe make a reference to last night. She still felt sick about what had happened, her stomach churning and rolling every time she thought about it, which was about every two minutes.

And she had an awful hangover, despite taking three aspirin. This morning, the throbbing in her head seemed as loud as her alarm clock. She'd woken up in her clothes from last night, except her shoes, which lay by her bedroom door. She couldn't remember too many details of the night before. She knew she and Aaron had fooled around. For the first time ever, she had passed out. That terrified her.

She gently rubbed her stomach, but that didn't calm her. As she walked through the hallway with Sienna, she envisioned herself slumped in the front passenger seat with her eyes closed and her legs open. There had been flashing lights. Had they been stopped by the police? She would have awoken for that, wouldn't she? She wasn't sure what those lights had been.

"Come on, Tracie, I'm starving," Sienna said next to her. Compared to Tracie, who could barely put one foot in front of the other, Sienna was practically skipping. On second thought, it wasn't just in comparison to her. Sienna looked happy today. Like the old Sienna, before Mark had broken up with her. She seemed downright cheery.

Tracie wasn't going to tell Sienna about Aaron. That would kill Sienna's mood fast. She'd get that look on her face where her lips pursed and her eyes narrowed, as if it was all she could do to hold back from screaming, *Tracie, you idiot! The guy's disgusting!* No, Tracie felt bad enough about making out with Aaron last night. Letting other people know, even her best friend, would humiliate her more.

What was up with Sienna? As she walked—bounced was more like it—she was actually whistling. "How you doing?" Tracie asked her.

"Great."

"Did you just go home last night?"

Sienna stopped whistling and her steps lost their bounce. "Last night," she repeated as if she was trying to figure something out.

"When you left the apartment complex with Carter." Did something happen between them? No, that was impossible. Tracie pushed the thought from her mind. Sienna was her best friend. She wouldn't go for Carter. No way.

Sienna shrugged, but it seemed like a deliberate, jerky move. Or maybe Tracie was just being paranoid. "When you guys headed for the Jacuzzi, it was still pretty early and Carter was thirsty," Sienna said. "So we went to Juice Caboose for a while."

"So what did Carter say? Anything about me?" Tracie asked. She knew she sounded needy, even desperate. But she didn't care.

"We mostly talked about school and stuff." Sienna sounded evasive.

"Stuff?"

"I don't know. Silly stuff." Sienna's lips had crept up. Was she aware that she was smiling?

Tracie dug her nails into her palm. Did something happen between her best friend and her ex-boyfriend?

She relaxed her hand. They wouldn't do that to her. She had a long history with each of them. Sienna and Carter were good-hearted and always loyal, probably the kindest people she knew.

"Oh, ick," Sienna said as they approached the cafeteria. "Aaron's got his hands all over Whitney Lowell again. Could his T-shirt be any tighter? It looks spray-painted on."

Tracie couldn't help looking at Aaron's table. He was sitting at his usual spot. Today, Whitney was on his lap. His hands appeared as if they were over her chest, but maybe that was just the way they were sitting.

"Don't even flatter that jerk by so much as glancing at him, or anywhere near him," Sienna warned her.

Too late. She had already looked in their direction. Aaron caught Tracie's gaze and winked at her. She quickly turned away.

"I can't believe that ass just winked at you," Sienna said. "Thank God you're not seeing him anymore."

Tracie nodded. How could she have fooled around with him last night? Merely thinking about it made her want a scalding shower with disinfectant soap.

"At least you had the good sense to dump him," Sienna continued. "For a while there, it seemed like his good looks had devoured your brain cells." They sat at their customary lunch table and took out their food. "So was the Jacuzzi fun?" Sienna asked her. "You didn't get caught, did you?"

"It was fun. We didn't get caught." Tracie knew she didn't sound very enthusiastic, but she couldn't talk about it. If Sienna ever found out what had happened with Aaron last night, she'd have zero respect for her.

Tracie already had lost all respect for herself. She stared at her turkey sandwich. She didn't feel like eating. Oh, why had she ever left Carter for Aaron? That was the stupidest decision of her entire life. "I can't believe I didn't get to be with Carter last night," she said.

Sienna choked a little on her sandwich. At least Sienna seemed to have an appetite.

"I thought we might even get back together," Tracie said. "But I should have known he wouldn't hop the fence to the Jacuzzi. He hates breaking rules." She sighed. "And that was my big chance to spend time with Carter. I don't have anything social planned until your birthday party next Friday."

The party! Of course! Sienna could invite Carter to the party—as Tracie's date. A night out on a fancy boat would be so romantic. She imagined herself standing on the bow of the yacht, wrapped in Carter's long arms, kissing under the bright moon as the waves lapped beneath them. She smiled at her friend, who was finishing her peanut butter sandwich. "Sienna, I have a great idea. Would you invite Carter to your party? I mean, ask him as my date."

"Oh, Tracie." Sienna dabbed her lips with a napkin. "I just called Carter about the Jacuzzi thing yesterday. Why don't you ask him?"

She stared at her uneaten lunch. "It would be so awful if he turned me down. At least if Carter says no to *you*, it won't be so humiliating. Please, Sienna? Just ask him to drive me to your party. I'll take it from there."

"I don't know. I don't want to keep bugging him," Sienna said.

"It won't bug him. And it's your party. You can invite anyone."

Sienna shrugged. "I guess."

"Thank you." Sienna was always helping her. Tracie owed her so much. But that's what best friends were for, right? Tracie nibbled at her sandwich. "Did Carter seem upset about leaving last night?"

Sienna stared at the lunch table for a long time. "We just didn't want to get caught trespassing," she finally said.

"I know," Tracie said. "I meant was Carter upset about leaving *me*?"

Sienna nodded. Tracie waited for her to say something, but she didn't.

"I'm so happy you're inviting Carter to your birthday party," Tracie said.

"I didn't ask him before because I thought it would be awkward for you."

"Oh, no, Sienna. It would be awkward coming alone." She had had a boyfriend since ninth grade and never realized how hard things were without one. Like last night, when everyone except her coupled off in the Jacuzzi. Or all those times when she didn't have a Saturday night date to look forward to, and had to console herself by drinking alone in her bedroom. She needed a boyfriend back in her life—namely, Carter. "When you invite Carter, you'll ask him to drive me there, right?" she asked Sienna. "And tell him I want to dance with him, okay?"

Sienna frowned.

"What's the matter?" Tracie asked her. "Aren't you excited about your party? It's going to be really cool, on that yacht your parents rented, with all the delicious food and the live music! I'm sure excited."

Sienna gave her a thin smile.

"You'll ask Carter, right?"

"Sure," Sienna said.

"If Carter comes back into my life, then I'll be happy again." Tracie wasn't sure who she was really trying to convince, Sienna or herself.

nine

After the bell rang, Tracie walked through the cafeteria next to Sienna, hoping that Aaron wouldn't confront her with Sienna nearby. But Sienna realized she'd forgotten a book from her locker and sped off, leaving Tracie alone.

Aaron rushed right over as if he'd been watching her, waiting for an opportunity to get her alone again. "Hey, gorgeous." He put his hand on her arm. His fingers lightly grazed her breast. "Come over after school today," he told her.

She slapped his hand away and turned to face him. "Leave me alone, Aaron," she said as assertively as she could.

"Uh-oh. You sound a lot different than you did last night. Did your bitchy friend bad-mouth me again?"

"Sienna?"

"I know she doesn't like me. When you're away from her, you're nice. Like when we were alone in my car." He put his arm around her, moved his hand to her bottom.

"Knock it off." She pushed his hand away.

"Yeah, Sienna got to you." He shook his head. "Did you tell her about last night? How happy I made you?"

"No, I didn't." She knew he'd bring it up. She just hoped he wouldn't tell anyone else. "Last night was a big mistake. I was really drunk. You took advantage of me."

"Ouch, Tracie." Aaron clutched his heart. "I'm hurt."

Tracie shook her head. "Sure you are."

"Admit it. We're hot together," Aaron said. "You don't realize how good you had it with me. I'm the best you'll ever have."

She took a step back. "God, just leave me alone. Please. I don't ever want to fool around with you again, Aaron. I don't even want to talk to you again. I wish I didn't even have to look at you again."

"You're worse than your bitchy best friend," he said.

Tracie rolled her eyes. "Whatever. Bye." She started to walk away.

"At least I have pictures to remember you by," he said.

"What?" She stopped and turned around.

Aaron was smirking. "Man, don't tell me you were so wasted you don't remember me taking pictures of you last night. Good quality too."

Oh, God. So that's what those flashing lights were. Her stomach churned more than ever now. It would serve him right to throw up all over him.

"I just wanted a little souvenir of our night together. You're so gorgeous, Tracie. And photogenic. Those pictures of you came out better than anything I could ever find online. If those pictures somehow ended up on the Net, they'd be getting thousands of hits a day."

"On the Net?" she exclaimed.

"Don't worry. I just took them for my own viewing pleasure. But I never realized how photogenic you are."

Was he blackmailing her? She would die if anyone saw pictures of her naked. She never would have let him take them in the first place if she'd been sober.

"Think about it, Tracie." Aaron moved close to her and put his arm around her again. This time she didn't move away. "Show me a little respect, and I'll show you some."

"I . . . I've got to go," she told him. His arm touching her body was making her more nauseated than ever.

Then someone else put his hand on her shoulder.

She flinched.

"Tracie." It was Mark. She slid away from Aaron and leaned into Mark. "Are you okay?" he asked her.

"Oh, Mark." Her voice quivered. "Not really."

"Get out of here, Aaron," he said. "Stay away from Tracie. You've done enough damage already."

"You don't know the half of it." Aaron leered at her. "See you soon," he said before walking off.

"What's wrong?" Mark asked Tracie.

It felt so good to have Mark here. But she couldn't tell him about last night.

People were rushing past them, hurrying to class. The last thing she wanted to do was make Mark late. So she said, "I'm okay. Don't worry. We'd better go to class now."

"Are you sure?" Mark asked.

She nodded. "Thanks for being here for me."

"Always," he said.

She stood on her tiptoes and kissed him on the cheek before rushing to class. Mark was there for her. Sienna was there for her too. But she couldn't tell either of them about Aaron.

She felt more alone than ever.

ten

If Lily weren't here, next to him at his keyboard, Mark probably would be banging his head against the wall of the garage. He had started writing a song, "Lover," weeks ago, and thought it had great potential; but something was off about it and he couldn't figure out what. Lily had been working with him on the song for almost an hour. They just couldn't get it right. They both liked how the lyrics turned out, but the tune was just okay, boring even. "Argh!" Mark said. "I feel so passionate about this song. I mean, it's about you, Lily, obviously. How could I not feel passionate? But I've tried everything, and that feeling isn't coming through in the music."

"Maybe we should take a break. It's Friday night. Let's go to a movie," Lily said.

Mark sighed. "That's so tempting. But Steve Guyda is dropping by in an hour, remember?"

"Why don't you tell him to come tomorrow instead?" Lily said.

"I can't ditch our new manager for a movie date."

"I wish your music career didn't take priority over me." She crossed her arms.

Not this argument again, Mark thought. Lily didn't appreciate his devotion to Amber Road. "It's *our* music career. It's your band too, Lily. And Sienna's and Tracie's and George's. We have a great future together, and I don't want to wreck it over a movie."

"A movie with your girlfriend on a Friday night."

"Lily. Please. We're going out tomorrow night."

She kept her arms crossed and didn't say anything. She was killing him with her silence.

He put his arm around her. "I'll even watch a chick flick with you if you want."

That seemed to do the trick. She nestled into him. "Can we go get facials first? Maybe a little shoe shopping too?" she asked.

"Sure." He grinned. "We can even throw in pedicures if you really want."

She giggled. "I'd love to get pedicures with you, but there's a limit to my cruelty."

He toyed with Lily's long, wavy hair. He loved that it felt so familiar to him now. "Sorry for acting so stressed tonight," he said. "Trying to figure out how to make 'Lover' work as a song is driving me nuts."

"I have an idea," Lily suggested. "Take off your clothes."

"What?" Lily was always coming up with wild ideas, but this might be her best one yet.

"Just do it," she said. "Don't worry, I'll join you."

"You want to have sex? Now? You know my family is home, Lily. What if they start banging on the door while—"

"We're not going to make love." She took off her shoes and her jeans, leaving them by her feet.

Mark had seen her naked many times, but her body never failed to amaze him. Wearing only thong underwear and a tank top made Lily's legs look even longer and more incredible than usual.

"Go ahead, Mark. Get undressed," she said.

So he took off his clothes too, keeping his eyes on Lily as she pulled off her tank top and threw it down, then slowly moved her thong down her legs. Man, she had a great body. "Lily, oh my God, Lily," he said, not caring who was in the house or about anything else. He tried to put his arms around her, but she stepped back.

"You feeling pretty passionate now?" she asked.

"Extremely."

"Good. Now you're in the right mood to fix that song." She took his hand and put it on the keyboard. "Your problem before was that you were thinking too much. Keep your hands on the keyboard, but play your passion."

"I don't know, Lily," he said.

She walked behind him and pressed her body against his and put her arms around him, resting her palms on his chest. He tried to turn around, but she said, "No. Play."

And he did. He stopped thinking about whether starting with a C note was right for the song, or whether the tempo was too fast, or how much bass was needed. Instead, he simply played his feelings, his passion for Lily, his girlfriend, his muse. The music came out sexy and different and perfect for a song called "Lover."

They wrote it all down, still naked. Mark knew they had created a fantastic song.

"We'd better get dressed. Unless you want to meet with your new manager in the nude. Steve Guyda should be coming soon," Lily said.

"Just one kiss first. Please. You're driving me crazy," he told Lily, and he held her tight and kissed her and wished they could make love right now.

But they got their clothes back on and smoothed their hair, and Guyda arrived just about a minute after they'd finished dressing. He greeted Mark with a pat on the back. "I have to say, when I signed you on I had some doubts about whether a group of high school kids could keep up with the big boys. But the manager of Waves told me that last night you rocked it like seasoned pros. I'm glad I can sniff out talent."

"We're really proving ourselves," Mark said.

"You bet," Guyda said. "And, Lily, you sing like an angel, but you've got a devilish look. It's a perfect combo in the rock biz."

"Thanks. I guess," Lily said.

"Now keep up that energy of yours on Monday when we'll be in the recording studio. Actually, you'll need your energy for more than just recording." Guyda reached into his briefcase and pulled out a large stack of promotional flyers and plastic bags filled with keychains and stickers he'd made with the band's name and website on it. He handed them to Mark. "I want you and your friends to put up these flyers all over San Diego and pass out the swag to anyone who likes music. I spent a lot of effort on setting up a fantastic MySpace site for you, so tell everyone you know about it. It's in big letters on the flyers. I'm going to schedule more dates for you to play at Waves," he said. "But you have to bring in a sizable crowd or you won't last long there."

"I think we're already building a small following," Mark said.

"You are, and that's good. But in this business, unfortunately, you need a big following," Guyda grumbled.

"Okay, we'll try our best to promote ourselves," Mark said. Guyda knew what he was talking about. Man, it felt good to have a pro like him on their side. Mark had managed the band before, but he was just an amateur, a high school student scrambling to do the best he could for Amber Road. Steve Guyda was the real deal.

Guyda had a reputation for being tough, Mark knew that. But he was also supposed to be excellent at his job. One of the bands Guyda had discovered was now touring Europe. Another had just signed with Columbia Records. So if he said Amber Road needed more promotion, Mark listened.

"I really like the vibe at Waves. I want us to keep playing there," Lily told Guyda.

"Yeah, we'd love to play there or anywhere else," Mark said. "Just remember next Friday night is out. It's Sienna's big eighteenth birthday party. Her parents rented a yacht and hired caterers and stuff."

Guyda frowned. "I blocked that out for you. But, listen. If you guys want a career, you really have to start accepting whatever club dates you're offered. Feel free to schedule as many parties as you want on Mondays. That's when a lot of clubs are closed."

"Who has a party on a Monday?" Lily complained.

Guyda's nostrils flared, making his nose ring seem more prominent. "Musicians dedicated to their work do." He closed his eyes for a moment. When he opened them, his face softened. "I know you kids are dedicated." His voice had softened too. "The first night I heard you, I was blown away by your talent. But it was more than that. I could practically sniff out the scent of ambition on you. I can tell you kids will work hard for success because you really want it."

Mark sure did. He wanted nothing more.

"Look," Guyda said. "I believe in you, in Amber Road. I wouldn't bust my ass for you kids otherwise. I've been schmoozing with Harry Darby, the club manager, to try to get you better time slots there. You guys with me or not?"

"Hell, yeah," Mark said. *We're professionals now,* he told himself. *We need to act like professionals and do whatever we can to make Amber Road a success.*

But Lily hadn't said a word. Her arms were crossed, as if she was completely *not* with Guyda.

Lily didn't care about Amber Road as much as he did. No one did. No one could. He never talked about it, but Amber Road was more than just a band. It was a way to remember Amber, to keep her alive.

"We're with you, Steve," Mark said. "We really appreciate everything you do for us."

"With that attitude, you'll be at the top of the charts before you know it." Guyda clapped Mark on the back. "Remember, success is a lot more about hard work than natural talent. You don't get to be a rock star by turning down gigs." He smiled. "I have some very good news for you. I got you a gig at The Spot a week from Saturday."

"The Spot! That's one of the best new clubs in San Diego," Mark said. "And on a weekend. Thanks!" He *knew* Guyda could take them places if they listened to him.

"I've been wanting to go to The Spot to listen to bands," Lily said. "I heard they picked, like, really talented groups. But I never thought my first time there I would actually be onstage. We've arrived!" she said. "With your help, of course, Steve."

"Well, you're getting there, but you haven't exactly arrived," he said. "For one thing, I've seen a lot bigger crowds at Waves than you got," Guyda continued. "It's a shame more people aren't getting the chance to find out how talented you all are. You really have to do more promo. That's why you really have to make good use of the promo stuff I brought over tonight. You have to draw people to your website and your MySpace site, put up flyers all over the place, do as much as you can to get people in the door."

"We tried," Lily said. "But we have school and—"

"School's important. But I know smart kids like you can get good grades *and* devote yourselves to your music careers," Guyda said. "You have a decent website, but it's like a ghost town. No one visits it. We're in the twenty-first century. Net promotion is key."

"I'd like to enjoy my senior year," Lily said. "I don't want to spend all my spare time trying to get more hits on our website."

"Hey, I want you to have fun too," Guyda said. "But isn't it fun to play your music in front of a crowd? I'm just trying to help you reach your goals, that's all. I want to earn my commission by giving you solid advice. After ten years in this industry, I know a little bit about what I'm talking about. Now, are you kids going to listen to your manager or what?"

Mark hated being called a kid. And being bossed around by Guyda was getting really old, really fast. But he didn't want to be one of those difficult musicians who people wouldn't work with. He took a deep breath, then told their manager, "You're the expert."

Guyda nodded. "With a little guidance, I see Amber Road going really far."

"Okay," Mark said. "You're our manager. You're supposed to manage us."

"And one more thing," Guyda continued.

Mark raised his eyebrows. He hoped it was a little thing.

"Don't worry. It's not a big thing," the manager said as if he were reading Mark's mind. "I want you to play more tunes people can rock to."

"Less ballads and slow stuff?" Lily asked.

Guyda shook his head once again. "Less indie stuff. More songs with an easy rhythm and simple lyrics. Your audience can't shout out the lyrics and dance to the music if the words and melodies are too complicated."

"You want us to tone down what we write?" Mark asked. "I don't know if that's even possible for me."

"No, no, no. Don't worry about that."

"Oh, good." Mark let out a long breath he realized he'd been holding since Guyda had criticized his songwriting. "Because you said you liked our songs," Mark said. "'Beautiful Girl,' 'Rock It Like a Rocket,' 'School's—' "

"They're terrific songs, really great." Guyda nodded encouragingly. "But you also need some that aren't so complex. Party songs. Dance tunes. You've heard of the band Daybreak, right?"

Mark nodded. Daybreak used to do commercial stuff— danceable, fun in a way, but totally unremarkable. "Are they still around?" he asked.

"They broke up about eight years ago, but people remember them. And do you know why? Daybreak plays tunes people can remember," Guyda said. "No fancy chords or anything. Catchy lyrics, with enough repetition the average fan can memorize them pretty quick. Everybody loves repetition."

"Steve, I don't think—" Mark started.

"You don't have to think," Guyda interrupted him. "You're the artist. As your manager, I'll do the thinking for you."

"Mark is smart enough to think for himself." Lily sounded like she was ready to murder Guyda or Mark, or both of them.

"You promised you'd listen to me," Guyda said.

Mark nodded. "Okay." His face felt tight. He wished he hadn't caved so easily.

"All right. Here are a bunch of songs Daybreak did." Guyda handed Mark a stack of sheet music and some tapes. "They really work. Your audience will be singing right along with you, having the time of their lives."

"But Steve—" Mark started to protest.

"Trust me. Learn the songs. Play a few of them at your next show. At the very least, give the new songs a try before you dismiss them outright."

Mark swallowed hard. "I guess that's fair."

"Just keep in mind that music is a business. Now I really got to go. I want to find a record producer to listen to you at The Spot next week. Congratulations again on a great show Thursday night, and I'll see you at the recording studio Monday." He left the garage.

Mark looked at Lily. The smile she'd worn before Guyda arrived had dissolved. He and Lily had been so happy a few minutes ago. How could one person—their own manager, for God's sake—manage to suck the spirit out of them so fast? Mark decided he'd better talk about things openly right now. "You okay with what Steve Guyda wants us to do?" he asked.

"Not really," she said.

"But, Lily," Mark said, "maybe our sound is a natural fit for Daybreak's songs. We should try them out, at least."

"But we just spent all that time working together, creating a fantastic song of our own. I don't like being told which songs I have to perform." She crossed her arms.

"Lily, come on," Mark pleaded.

"I think we'd better call it a night." She walked out of the garage.

"Please," Mark called after her, but she didn't even slow down.

eleven

Tracie pushed aside her taco combo plate. "How can I be so exhausted on a Saturday afternoon at the mall? It's not like I even bought anything today."

Across the table from her at the food court, Sienna said, "Let me take a wild guess. Because you've shopped at half the stores here, promoted Amber Road all day, and tried on about fifty dresses?"

"Oh, yeah." Tracie giggled. "I just want to look great for Carter at your party."

Sienna ate another forkful of salad. She hadn't seen Tracie so wonderfully hopeful in a long time. "We'll get you a perfect dress," Sienna said, "one that will put Carter into cardiac arrest. You'll have to revive him with mouth-to-mouth."

"I don't know if there is a perfect dress. I've already tried on so many dresses," Tracie complained.

"The perfect dress for you is out there, I know it," Sienna said. "We'll find it, even if we have to go to every store in this mall, and every mall in San Diego."

Sienna already had gotten her own party dress. She'd shopped at the mall by herself about a week ago and bought the second dress she'd tried on, a Nicole Miller from Nordstrom. She thought it was beautiful, white and floor-length like a Greek goddess would wear, with a tight bodice that showed off her cleavage. Too bad there was no guy in her life to appreciate it. *I like what I look like in the dress,* Sienna told herself. *That's what matters the most.* She wasn't sure whether she totally believed that, but it sounded good.

Tracie slumped in her chair. "You have so much energy, Sienna."

"I'm on a mission." Sienna smiled. "We should also put up some more flyers this afternoon promoting Amber Road."

Tracie nodded. "Otherwise, we'll have to incur the wrath of Steve Guyda. God, we sure have a hardass manager."

"He can't be mad at us after today. We did so much for Amber Road. Taping up flyers by the pay phone and in the ladies' room and at half the restaurants at the food court."

"And don't forget flirting," Tracie said.

Sienna grinned. "Flirting is hard work." They had flirted with a greasy-haired guy at the music store and a sophomore at EB Games to encourage them to pass out flyers and Amber Road keychains and stickers to their customers. "Do you ever look at the CDs in the music store and imagine where ours would be if we made it big?" Sienna asked.

"Only every single time I'm there," Tracie said.

"Me too," Sienna said. "There are a lot of other rock groups that start with the letter *A*."

Tracie smiled. "I noticed that too today. I'm too pooped to even eat my shrimp taco." Tracie slid it over to Sienna.

"No wonder you're so thin. I never lose my appetite. That's why I'll never be a size three like you." Sienna tasted the taco. "Yum!"

"Oh, Sienna, you look great," Tracie said. "I just wish there were a magical dress that would make Carter want to get back together with me."

Sienna patted her friend's hand on the table. "You don't need magic, girl. I bet once he sees you all primped out and remembers how sweet and smart you are, he'll be dying to have you back."

They spent another hour shopping before they finally found a dress for Tracie. It cost more than four hundred dollars, but it was a good-quality Tocca, one of Tracie's favorite brands. "It's perfect," Sienna said as Tracie came out of the dressing room and looked at herself from all angles in the three-way mirror. The dress was stunning—the same turquoise as Tracie's eyes and clingy in all the right places, with a halter top that made her look voluptuous but still classy, and a hemline high above her knees to show off her shapely legs.

"You think this will get Carter's attention?" Tracie asked.

"If it doesn't, it means he's blind. Or gay. Or dead. Actually, I think he'd have to be all three not to notice how beautiful you look in it." Sienna laughed.

"I'll take it," Tracie said. "I never thought I'd say this, but I'm tired of shopping."

"You? Tired of shopping? Now I'm really worried about you," Sienna joked. Tracie giggled.

Sienna didn't know if it was the new gorgeous dress or the hopes that went with it, or maybe a combination of both, but Tracie acted like her old happy self again. As Sienna drove away from the mall, the two girls sang along to the radio and Tracie played air guitar. "I wonder who's more excited about your birthday party," Tracie said, "you or me?" She laughed. "God, I wish I could see Carter right now. I hate to wait six more days for us to be together. Sienna, I really think Carter and I are meant for each other."

"Maybe you could accidentally bump into him after school on Monday. You could suggest going for a drive," Sienna suggested.

"Accidentally?" Tracie shook her head. "He'd see through that so fast. Besides, he always has activities after school. Swim team, student council meetings, all that."

"Hmm." Sienna thought for a moment. "You could ask him for help on your homework."

"He'd probably just help me with it over the phone. Or we'd sit at his kitchen table with his mother hanging over us." Tracie sighed. "I guess I just have to wait until Friday night."

"Hold on. Don't give up." Sienna grinned at Tracie. "Remember, I'm on a mission to get you and Carter back together. Let's form a plan. You should do something fun with him tonight, where you can laugh and have a good time and forget about the problems you two had the last few months. We could get a group together."

"But if too many people are around, I might hardly talk to him," Tracie said. "Plus, it's hard to organize a group at the last minute."

Sienna shrugged. "Why don't you just ask him somewhere yourself?"

"But then it'll seem like I want to go on a date with him," Tracie said.

But you do want to go on a date with him! Sienna wanted to yell. Instead, she stared ahead at the road. She was trying to help, but all Tracie could do was knock down every idea she had, without coming up with a single one of her own. *It's not really her fault,* Sienna told herself. *Tracie is naturally pessimistic. It's just her personality.* Sienna thought some more. "You could pretend you got free tickets to somewhere fun. Sea World?"

"That's more of a daytime thing. I'm hoping to see him tonight."

As Sienna neared Tracie's house, she felt relieved that Tracie would be getting out of her car soon.

"You go out with us too, okay?" Tracie asked her. "We can pretend we got three free tickets to something."

Sienna shrugged.

"Please?"

"Okay," she said. *But Tracie can come up with her own idea for a change*, Sienna thought. *I'm done having all my ideas shot down.* She parked at the curb by Tracie's house. Tracie stayed in the car, frowning.

After a couple of minutes, Sienna couldn't stand it anymore. She tossed out another suggestion. "How about a movie? We actually do have free tickets. Remember when the power went out five minutes into that Cameron Diaz movie?"

Tracie shook her head. "That was a long time ago, last summer, I think. I already used my free ticket."

There she went, knocking her ideas again. Sienna didn't give up. "I used my ticket too, but Carter doesn't have to know that."

Finally, Tracie grinned and said, "Oh, you're good."

"We could see something funny to make you laugh together, or a horror movie so you could snuggle next to each other," Sienna said.

"Yeah, and it would be really dark in there."

"You'll sit in the middle, between me and Carter," Sienna said.

"I love it!" Tracie exclaimed. "And we can go out for dinner afterward too."

"Great idea," Sienna said. "I'll give some excuse why I can't make it. We'll take separate cars to the movie theater so I can drive myself home afterward."

"It'll be like a date, but a stealth date." Tracie giggled. "Ooh, I hope Carter can go."

Sienna smiled at her. "Me too. You should call him now before you chicken out." Sienna hated to lie to such a nice, honest guy. But Tracie was dying to see him, and Sienna had to put her best friend first.

So Tracie took out her cell phone. "This could be it," she said as she pressed Carter's number. "The night we get back together."

twelve

Carter didn't seem exactly ecstatic to hear from Tracie, but he acted friendly enough as they chatted for a minute.

Finally, next to her in the car, Sienna mouthed, "Ask him."

So Tracie told Carter oh so casually, "I have these movie passes to the theater in Solana Beach." She added, "And they're going to expire. I thought we could catch a flick tonight."

"Tonight?" He said it as if she'd just asked him to clean her bathroom.

"It'll be fun," she said in a fake-peppy voice. "Sienna's coming too."

"Oh, Sienna's coming." After a pause, he said, "Okay. What time should I meet you at the movie theater?"

Tracie felt her whole body relax as soon as he said yes. But once she hung up the phone and had a minute to think about their conversation, she told Sienna, "Carter agreed to come only after he found out we wouldn't be alone."

Sienna reached over and patted her shoulder. "He's probably just nervous about being on an official date with you. He might have to be eased into rebuilding your relationship."

"Maybe," Tracie said. "I hope that's what it is, anyway. Well, I'd better get ready." She opened the car door. "Thanks a lot for going with us tonight."

"No problem," Sienna said. "You guys were good together. I want to see you two happy again."

Tracie rushed up her driveway and into her house. She wanted to look great for Carter, but she didn't want to appear as if she'd put a lot of effort into it. She took out half the sweaters from her bedroom drawers before choosing one she'd bought a couple of months ago. It was pink cashmere to emphasize sweetness and softness, but also snug to show off her body. The jeans she chose were so tight she could barely pull up the zipper. They made her butt look pert and rounded. She wore gold chandelier earrings and a matching necklace Carter had given her for Christmas, applied light pink lipstick and a heavy dose of mascara and rouge, and, after trying on five pairs of shoes, decided on black platform sandals. Pretending to appear as if she just threw on any old clothes and rushed out the door was often more time-consuming than looking put-together.

All that prep time made Tracie twenty minutes late getting to the movie theater. She knew Carter hated when she was late, but she thought it was more important to look her best than to be on time.

Sienna and Carter were waiting for her in front of the theater, laughing about something. Sienna was still wearing the long-sleeve polo shirt and khakis she had on at the mall today. Carter looked good in a button-down shirt and dark jeans.

"What are you guys laughing at?" Tracie asked.

"Carter was just doing a hilarious imitation of Miss Vile Viola, our English teacher," Sienna said, still chuckling.

"Oh, let me hear," Tracie said.

"You really have to be in our class to get it," Carter said.

"Yeah," Sienna said. "The only good thing about my being stuck in Miss Vile's class is getting to hear you mimic her."

"So, you already got tickets?" Tracie gestured to the movie tickets dangling from Sienna's hand.

"Well, you were twenty minutes late," Carter pointed out, as if that were a felony or something.

"How much do I owe you?" Tracie asked Sienna.

Carter cocked his head. "I thought you girls had free passes."

"Oh, right," Tracie said. "So what are we seeing?"

"*Mon Cousin, Mon Amour*," Sienna said. "It's supposed to be great."

"Are you kidding? A French movie?" Tracie rolled her eyes. "With subtitles, right?"

"The *San Diego Reader* loved it," Carter said.

"That's the review I read. It's supposed to have subtle, ironic humor," Sienna said. "That sounds like just my kind of thing."

"Mine too," Carter said.

Tracie crossed her arms. "Maybe you guys should see it together and I should watch something else."

"Don't be like that, Tracie," Sienna said. "Just because it has subtitles doesn't mean it's not funny. Some of my favorite funny movies are foreign."

"Did you ever see *Amélie*?" Carter asked.

"I own it," Sienna said.

"Oh, wow. How about *Tampopo*?"

"The Japanese comedy about the noodle house? I love that movie," Sienna said. "You're the first person I ever met who saw that too."

Tracie wondered if they'd even notice if she walked away.

"Tracie, I told you *Tampopo* was good. I wish I could have convinced you to watch it with me," Sienna said.

"Tracie doesn't like foreign movies," Carter said.

"You just need to give them a chance, Tracie. You'll like this one, I bet." Sienna smiled at her. "Let's go in so we can get good seats."

Sienna and Carter walked into the theater with Tracie trailing after them. Carter headed to the snack bar. "I'm buying," he said. "What do you girls want?"

"You know what I want," Tracie said. Had he forgotten already what she always ordered? They must have seen close to a hundred movies together while they were dating.

"I wasn't sure if you still liked diet soda and licorice," he said.

"I still do." She smiled at him. "I'm glad you remembered."

"I'll have a regular soda and a small popcorn," Sienna said.

"How about we get a large and share?" Carter asked.

"Tracie doesn't like popcorn," Sienna said.

"I know. I was talking about sharing with you," he said.

Sienna mumbled, "Okay, I guess," and Tracie clutched her churning stomach. She and Sienna had planned a stealth date for tonight. She just hadn't realized the date would be between Carter and Sienna.

They got their snacks and took their seats. Of course, Carter and Sienna had to sit together because they were sharing popcorn. Tracie sat on the other side of Carter, but it didn't really matter. It wasn't as if he held her hand in the theater or even whispered to her. He was too busy laughing along with Sienna at the movie's dumb French jokes.

Maybe if she hadn't been so upset, she would have found the jokes funny too. It was hard to concentrate with Carter right next to her, and, worse, Sienna right next to him. How could she focus on the subtitles and the humorous irony or whatever when she was wondering whether Carter's and Sienna's hands were touching inside the popcorn box?

She settled on laughing whenever Carter and Sienna laughed. And she put her forearm on the armrest between Carter and her, hoping he'd make contact with her. But he avoided her.

About an hour into the movie, she heard the popcorn box drop to the ground. She breathed a little easier. There was no excuse for Carter and Sienna to touch each other now.

She sneaked a peek at them. Carter's arm was on the arm-rest he shared with Sienna. What a jerk! They started laughing again, so Tracie faked another laugh, though she felt more like crying.

When the movie was finally over and they were walking toward the lobby, Sienna turned to her and asked, "What did you think?"

I think you should get away from Carter! she wanted to shout. But she controlled herself. "The movie was pretty good," she said.

"Pretty good? It was great!" Carter said. "Maybe the best movie I've seen this year. Don't you agree, Sienna?"

Sienna nodded.

They walked outside. This was supposed to be her cue to ask Sienna and Carter if they wanted to get something to eat, but she felt so bummed she just wanted to go home.

Sienna stopped before they got to the parking lot, and stared at Tracie, apparently waiting for her to suggest going out to a restaurant.

Carter stopped too. "You girls want to get something to eat?"

Well, Tracie told herself, *at least I don't have to ask tonight.*

"I'm going home," Sienna said. "I'm full from all that popcorn."

"You should sit with us anyway and just get an iced tea or something," Carter told her.

"Thanks, but I'd better leave," Sienna said. "But Tracie, you didn't eat that much. You should go out with Carter."

"I'd love to," Tracie forced herself to say. But she really just wanted this awful evening to be over.

"You sound tired," Carter said. "It's okay. I'm pretty tired too. We'll do it another time. I'm parked over there." He pointed to the left.

"We're parked on the other side," Sienna said. "See you later."

As he walked away, Tracie gave him a small wave. Then Sienna shouted, "Bye!" and he turned around and gave Sienna a huge smile. Tracie couldn't remember the last time he'd smiled at *her* like that.

Once he left, Sienna asked, "Why didn't you go out to eat with him, Tracie? You could have been alone with him."

"He doesn't want to be alone with me," Tracie said. "I think he'd rather be alone with you, actually."

"Oh, come on." Sienna shook her head.

"You guys were gushing over each other all night," Tracie said. "Ooh, we see the same movies! Ooh, we both like popcorn! Ooh, we laugh at the same jokes! Ooh, ooh, ooh!"

"Just because we're both into foreign films—"

"Why did you choose that movie anyway?" Tracie asked her. "You know I don't like subtitles."

Sienna hunched her shoulders. "I thought you might like a funny movie that got great reviews. If you'd met me at the theater when you said you would—"

"So now it's my fault." Her voice had gotten too loud. People congregating around the movie theater were starting to give her strange looks. She lowered her voice. "I'm a little late, so you decide to pick a movie you know I'll hate."

"Oh, Tracie, come on," Sienna said. "I didn't think that."

"Well, it was a bad idea to meet him here." She had to consciously keep her voice down.

"Maybe it *was* a bad idea. I'm sorry," Sienna said. "I was trying to help you, that's all."

Tracie sighed. She shouldn't make Sienna the scapegoat. Sienna *had* been trying to help her tonight. She, Tracie, had been the one who wanted to see Carter tonight, who asked Sienna to come with her. Just because it didn't work out didn't make it Sienna's fault.

Sienna put an arm around her. "So Carter and I both like foreign films and popcorn. That doesn't mean anything. You two dated for three years. You obviously had a spark."

"*Had* a spark?" Tracie asked.

"*Have* a spark, I guess," Sienna said. "More than a spark. A flame. A wildfire."

"I sure hope so," Tracie said.

"He'll realize it soon. Maybe at my birthday party. Things probably will be a lot different there," Sienna said. "You'll be all dressed up, and you'll drive over together in his car, just the two of you. It'll be a real date, very romantic."

"You think so?" Tracie asked her.

"I do."

Tracie bit her lip. "I'm sorry for blaming you tonight, Sienna. It wasn't your fault. I feel bad, after you spent half the day waiting for me while I tried on a zillion dresses, and you were doing me a favor tonight."

"I shouldn't have picked that movie. That was a mistake. I'm sorry too. You know what?" Sienna went on. "It's not that late. As long as we're at the theater, we could buy more tickets and go see that Jennifer Aniston film that's playing here."

"In English, right?" Tracie asked.

Sienna laughed. "Definitely."

"Then that sounds great," Tracie said. And they got in line for tickets.

thirteen

Mark looked at his watch. Everyone from Amber Road except Lily was in his garage. She was ten minutes late on a day when they had a lot to do. Not only did they need to rehearse their set and prepare for tomorrow's session at the recording studio, but they had to learn some of the new songs Steve Guyda had given them and figure out how to promote the band better.

"I don't want to spend my Sunday afternoon waiting for Lily," Sienna said.

"We could start without her," Tracie suggested.

Mark nodded. "Okay, I guess." But Amber Road just wasn't the same without Lily. She made it feel special. She made *him* feel special.

There was a knock on the door connecting the garage to the house, and Mark rushed to open it. His whole body tensed when he saw Aaron facing him, with Lily behind him. Mark thought he heard Tracie gasp.

"What are you doing here?" Mark didn't bother to sound polite.

Aaron turned to Lily. "Who does your boyfriend think he is? A cop?"

Mark took a breath to calm himself. As much as he disliked Aaron, he didn't want to argue with his girlfriend's brother. "You're at my house, dude, that's all. I was curious," he said.

"If you must know, I was doing my twin sister a favor by driving her over. Just like I did Tracie a favor a few nights ago and drove *her*." He peered in the garage. "Right, Tracie? You liked that favor."

There was no response. Mark glanced at Tracie, cowering against the wall of the garage. He wondered if something had happened between Aaron and her on the way back from the Jacuzzi. Man, he hoped not.

"Where is Tracie? She here?" Aaron tried to look into the garage again.

"That's none of your business." Mark blocked the doorway, and hopefully Aaron's line of vision. Forget about being nice to Lily's twin brother! The guy was a jerk. Mark remembered how upset Tracie had been with Aaron at school on Friday. She didn't seem much better today. He hoped she was okay.

He looked past Aaron, at Lily. How could she have let her brother come here? "Lily. If you needed a ride, you could have asked me."

"But Aaron—"

"Aaron is not allowed at band rehearsals," Mark said gruffly. "He upsets Tracie, makes Sienna mad, and gets everyone distracted."

Aaron leaned in to see the rehearsal space. "Tracie didn't seem very upset the other—"

"Shut up!" Tracie shouted.

"Get the hell out of here," Mark said.

"Fine. I've got better things to do than watch Lily waste her talent with you small-time wannabes." Aaron turned around and walked away.

Lily stomped into the garage. Mark had never seen her like this, so angry. Usually she acted carefree. "Listen, Mark," she said. "Don't insult my brother."

"Lily, he doesn't belong at rehearsals." Mark tried to sound calm, but his heart was pounding. For the thousandth time, he wished Aaron and Lily weren't related. He took a deep breath. "It's hard to focus on our music with your brother here," he told Lily, as if Aaron were merely a minor distraction.

Lily sneered, looking at that moment frighteningly like her twin. "You treat the band like it's the only thing that matters in life."

Mark moved closer to her. "Lily, you matter. You matter so much to me."

She put her elbow out to prevent him from coming any closer. "You say you love me, but it's Amber Road you love. And not just the band. The girl Amber too."

He loved Lily, but he couldn't stand hearing her right now, the way she said Amber's name, her voice filled with disgust. He glanced at the others. Sienna had her arm around Tracie, who looked shaken up. George was staring at his sheet music. There was a long, uncomfortable silence.

Finally, George cleared his throat. "Amber Road's a good name, but I'd like to propose a change. Let's rename the band after one of the greatest musicians of all time—me. We'll call ourselves George Road."

Mark smiled. "How modest you are."

"Wait. I have something even better. Drumroll, please." He beat his drum, then said, "How about George Rules? Or George Rocks."

"How about George Reeks?" Sienna shouted out.

Everyone laughed. Mark mouthed, "Thanks," to George for diverting the tension between Lily and him. "How about we think up new ways to promote ourselves now?" Mark suggested. "Guyda said we need to do a lot more."

George snapped his fingers. "I know how we can get a ton of publicity."

"Good, George, let's hear," Mark said.

"Murder our manager."

The girls giggled. Mark shook his head.

"Seriously, Guyda's right about us needing to promote ourselves more. Hardly anyone's visiting our website," George said. "I think most of our website hits come from us checking how many hits we get."

"We need to bring new people in to hear our music. Maybe try a different venue," Mark said.

"We could perform at the mall," Tracie suggested.

"Now you're talking! I'll use any excuse to go to the mall," Sienna said. "And we could hand out our CDs and flyers too."

"That sounds like a great plan," Mark said. "Let's talk to Guyda about setting something up. We should get started on rehearsal now. Tomorrow's the big day at the recording studio, and next weekend is our show at The Spot. And, like I wrote in my e-mail to you guys, I promised Steve Guyda we'd learn a few of Daybreak's songs. Did you see the songs I attached to the e-mail? Which ones do you like best?"

Lily rolled her eyes. "None of them."

Mark wasn't exactly excited about them either. On paper and on the tape he'd listened to, they seemed trite and dull. But maybe the songs would be a lot better when Amber Road performed them. The band could try to make the songs their own. "I think 'Surf's Up' seems like one of the better ones," Mark said. "And George, you probably love it because you're a surfer."

"Love to surf, don't love the song," George said.

"Come on. Let's try it," Mark urged.

So they did. It wasn't bad. The refrain, "Surf's up, and it's calling me," sounded all right. The first few times. But it repeated so much, Mark quickly tired of singing it and Sienna said she thought she lost a couple of brain cells just listening to it. "I hope I can get it out of my head," Tracie said.

"Let's hope you can't," Mark said. "Let's hope no one can forget it. A memorable song is a good thing, you know."

"Not if you remember it for the wrong reasons," Sienna said.

"I'll remember it like I remember that time I had food poisoning," Lily said.

Mark laughed at that, but Lily didn't even smile.

Mark had the band learn one other song from Daybreak, "I'm So into You I Don't Know What to Do." He thought the meter was sloppy and the lyrics juvenile, but he didn't say so. Everyone else was negative enough about it.

"Okay, we tried a couple of songs, like Guyda asked us to," Lily said. "Now can we get to our own stuff? I need to get the bad-song taste out of my mouth."

"I can't wait," Tracie said. "I never knew what a great songwriter Mark was until I had to play Daybreak's stuff."

They agreed to practice "Right Beside Me," one of the first songs Mark had written for Amber Road. He had never seen the group so eager to rehearse. And their enthusiasm was justified. When they sang "Right Beside Me," everything felt true and good again. Mark's worries about his argument with Lily, the pressure he felt from Steve Guyda, his concerns about whether they'd be ready to play at The Spot on Saturday—all his troubles left him as he got carried away by the words he'd carefully crafted, and heard Lily's scorching voice belt out the lyrics in a wide range of notes, and George tackling the complicated drumming they'd worked so hard on, and Tracie and Sienna playing their guitars almost as if they were one person with four hands.

The group went right on to "Don't Leave" and "Stray Cat" and then "Kiss Me," playing with only a few seconds between songs, shifting with the moods in each one, on a roller coaster of emotion. Afterward, they were breathless. They hugged each other without speaking, as if they'd gone through an important experience together.

With the songs Guyda had given them, they were just keeping up. But with their own songs, especially the most complex ones like "Right Beside Me," they were searching inside themselves. They were living the songs with their hearts and souls, and the songs became a part of them. "Damn, we're amazing," Mark said.

"With the right music we are," Lily said. "We shouldn't have wasted our time on Daybreak's songs. Steve Guyda is our manager, not our dictator."

True. But many of Guyda's bands had become big successes, and Guyda already had been getting Amber Road steady, paying gigs. "We don't have to play the songs onstage," Mark said. "All we lost is some of our time. And we probably gained the respect of Steve Guyda by at least trying the songs."

"I like trying *our* new songs," Tracie said. "Doing our own stuff makes us unique."

"We worked hard writing those songs," Lily added.

She was right. For each song, it had taken hours to find the right notes on the keyboard, translate the sounds to musical instruments, and create the perfect lyrics to fit the music while making a statement. After they wrote the songs, they had to teach them to the other members of the band. Everyone had to learn the words and music, and practice over and over until they not only had the song down but put a cool and unique spin on it. Often the song evolved from something good to something great as they developed it in rehearsal.

Now Guyda wanted them to throw away their efforts just because he believed people would be too lazy or stupid or set in their ways to want to discover music that wasn't totally simple and mainstream.

Mark thought he was wrong. But he also recognized that as a seasoned, successful manager, his decisions should be respected. Trying to defend Guyda to his bandmates, Mark said, "A lot of bands mix in some pop songs with the more personal stuff."

"You used to call those bands sellouts," Sienna said.

Mark flinched. She had a good point. But someone had to take Guyda's position. "Steve Guyda is one of the best band managers in San Diego," Mark said. "He knows what he's doing. When we were on our own, we felt lucky to play high school dances. With Guyda managing us, we're performing at Waves and The Spot. People are hearing our music. Isn't that what we want?"

Lily frowned. "I guess."

Mark wished she'd take his side, but Lily did whatever she wanted. She couldn't be swayed. "We can still do our own stuff," Mark said. "Let's do 'Beautiful Girl' now." Because they wrote the song together, singing it always set off sparks between them. Maybe it was just what was needed to put Lily in a good mood again.

But Lily sounded strained during the duet. She seemed to have to work at the song. Her voice hit the right notes but lacked passion. Mark hoped she would get it back. Not just for the sake of the band, but for him.

fourteen

Mark waited outside the recording studio on Monday after school. He was early for their session. He'd been awake before five this morning, way too excited to sleep. It was hard to believe the band was going to record songs in a professional studio.

George and a new girl, Emily, arrived soon after Mark. The three of them joked around as they stood waiting for the others. Emily was pretty, with soft, wavy blonde hair and hazel eyes, her plump body dressed casually in a short-sleeved blouse and jeans. She seemed nice enough. Had George finally found himself a normal girl?

A siren sounded. A police car sped toward them, pulled to the curb, and stopped.

Mark's stomach took a plunge. "I wonder what's wrong," he murmured.

Emily started running down the street. Two police officers chased after her, shouting, "Stop! We have a warrant for your arrest, Emily Barnes." They were able to catch up with her and handcuff her. As one of the officers put Emily in the back of the police car, he said, "We have six witnesses to that robbery you pulled off last month."

"Which one?" she asked before the officer closed the car door.

As they drove away, George shrugged and said, "She seemed like a nice girl. A little evasive, but who knew?"

Mark shook his head.

Sienna and Tracie arrived a minute later, and Lily drove in right behind them. Mark's heart pounded as Lily approached the recording studio. *Please don't be upset with me,* he begged silently. He smiled with false bravado and looked at the three girls in turn. "Isn't this exciting!"

Lily smiled back at him. "I'm totally into this."

Phew. He took that to mean Lily wasn't mad anymore, or at least was attempting to forgive him. He rushed over and put his arm around her.

Steve Guyda sped toward him. He was always in a hurry. His intensity made Mark, who had always thought of himself as a type A, feel like a slacker. "This is it," Guyda said as he neared the group. "Now I can let producers hear your fantastic sound at its best. Let's get started."

Guyda punched some numbers on the studio door's keypad and opened it. "Hey, J.J.! Benny!" he called out. "I'm bringing that band I told you about. Be prepared to be blown away!"

After everyone walked in, he closed the door behind him and said, "Go ahead. Familiarize yourselves with the space. Time is money here, so we need to get a move on."

But they remained standing at the door, taking it all in together, peering openmouthed inside the recording studio. This was their first time in a professional studio and it was awesome. Top-quality instruments, probably with a combined worth of over one hundred thousand dollars, were set up for them on one side of the giant room. In the corner was a small vocal booth with headphones for Lily. On the other side, separated by a huge plate-glass window, was the control room. Two skinny guys wearing headphones stood there among microphones and a ton of buttons and gears and other expensive-looking high-tech gear. Everything looked new and sophisticated and state of the art.

"Time is money," Guyda said again. "Come on. Make sure the instruments are tuned before we start."

They headed for the recording area and picked up the instruments. "I can't believe I get to play these drums. They make my set look like a toy," George said.

Mark ran his hand over the electronic keyboard and tested it out. There were so many knobs and switches on it. He bet this baby could do anything. Compared with the one here, his keyboard at home seemed like a relic. "I'm going to make sounds you guys have never heard before," he announced with a smile.

"And they should be crystal clear," their manager said. "The quality of these instruments is phenomenal. Why don't you start playing 'Beautiful Girl'? You're going to love how good it sounds with the right instruments." He pointed to Lily. "Go over to the vocal booth and put the headphones on." Then he turned to the men in the control room. "J.J., Benny, you ready for them?"

One of the guys used his thumb and index finger to make an "Okay" sign. Mark called out, "Three, two, one, rock!" And they did.

It was phenomenal. Guyda was right. Using high-quality instruments made a big difference. But it wasn't just that. It was the excitement of being in a recording studio, crafting a performance not just for today, but for the future, that possibly could be heard by hundreds if not thousands of people. For Mark, it was also that he was so grateful Lily wasn't upset with him anymore, that she was here, singing the song they'd started creating together on the beach and then finished at his house. Though it was called "Beautiful Girl," he'd always thought of it as "Lily's Song."

After they finished, Guyda said, "That was magnificent. Later today we'll record the vocals and instruments separately and try a few variations of the song, but I really don't think it's possible for you kids to improve on that rendition. It's times like right now I'm proud to be your manager."

"Thanks, man," Mark said. "This is so cool. Without you managing us, we never would have felt ready to be in a recording studio today. This is so exciting, and this keyboard is unreal. I can't wait to perform 'School's Out' on this." He played with the keys.

"Oh, yeah. My drum solo's going to be amazing," George said.

"Actually, I changed a few things," Guyda said. "You won't be recording 'School's Out' today."

Mark felt his brows furrow. "I thought we were doing 'School's Out' and 'Candy' after 'Beautiful Girl.' "

"Your 'Beautiful Girl' was excellent, but it's better for you to be recording the new songs right now," Guyda said. "Trust me. You can make 'Surf's Up' your own. It's great as it is, and you'll improve it. I bet you'll be terrific at 'I'm So into You' too."

"We can make our *own* songs our own," Lily protested. "Mark's written so many great songs."

Guyda shook his head. "I can't manage you kids if you're going to argue with my decisions."

Mark hated when Guyda called them *kids*, but there were more important things to worry about. Like being allowed to record only one of their own songs.

"As I explained before," Guyda said, "with a new teen band, people don't want music that's too tricky. It's common for young bands to do simple songs. Now that we've eaten up more valuable studio time, are you going to let me lead you or not?"

"Not," Lily said.

Mark loathed conflict—especially when he was in the middle of it and his band manager was pitted against his girl-friend. But he felt that he had to do what was best for Amber Road, and that Guyda knew more than Lily and him about making a band successful. "Lily, we wouldn't even be here in the recording studio without Steve Guyda's help," he told her. "And we did get to record 'Beautiful Girl.' How about we give the other songs a try?"

Lily glared at Mark as if she was ashamed to be his girlfriend.

"Come on, kids. I'm just trying to make you successful," Guyda said. "That's what you hired me for, isn't it?"

Mark nodded.

"Let's go then. Time is money," Guyda said.

And really, the songs came out all right once they recorded them. Mark thought "Beautiful Girl" was the best by far, maybe because everyone in the band was so passionate about it, or maybe just because it was a damn fine original song. But the other songs sounded good also.

Their manager seemed very pleased. "I knew there was a reason I wanted to represent you," Guyda told them as they left the recording studio together. "Remember I said you kids were booked at The Spot on Saturday night?" he asked.

"Yeah, so?" Lily had her arms crossed.

"So it's really cool," Tracie said.

"You know weekend slots are coveted," Guyda said.

"I love being coveted," George said.

"Guess what headliner you're opening for," Guyda said.

"I give up. Tell us." Lily rolled her eyes.

"Platinum Card."

"Holy crap! Really?" Sienna said.

Guyda nodded.

"Awesome," Mark said. Platinum Card was one of the hottest bands in San Diego. They were on the brink of national stardom.

"Dudes, we're going to be rock stars! And, Steve, you're the man!" George gave everyone high-fives, and soon they were high-fiving each other and whooping and cheering, though Lily just smiled thinly while her arms remained crossed.

"Man, you're a good manager," Mark told Guyda.

"And we're good musicians and singers. The greatest manager in the world couldn't book us unless we were good in the first place," Lily said.

"You want to go out tonight and celebrate?" Mark asked her. "Just the two of us?"

She looked away. "Not tonight. Honestly, I don't think being sellouts is cause for celebration."

"We're not sellouts. We're just trying to break in," Mark told her.

She rolled her eyes. He obviously hadn't convinced her. He wasn't sure whether he'd convinced himself either.

fifteen

Sienna sneaked a peek at the clock on the classroom wall. Still thirty-four minutes to go. And it was only Tuesday. She was so excited about her party and playing at The Spot this weekend, she didn't know how she could survive the week. Usually, she liked English. In fact, she loved reading novels. But this year she had Miss Viola, the world's most boring teacher, and this week they were focusing on poetry. Not the poetry itself—but the *form* of poetry. As if knowing the meaning of onomatopoeia would ever come in handy in real life.

She felt his gaze on her again. It was weird that she knew when he was looking at her. Maybe it was because he did it so often these days. She turned her head. Sure enough, Carter, who sat in her row but with someone between them, was staring right at her and smiling again.

She returned his smile and then gave him a tiny wave.

Stop it, you're flirting, Sienna reprimanded herself and looked down at her desk. She owed it to her best friend to keep away from him.

She still felt his eyes directed on her. Though she dared not look at him, she knew his eyes were beautiful, light blue flecked with bits of gray, and warm and bright. Maybe if her teacher weren't such a bore, she could focus on something besides Carter and his eyes.

She still needed to find a way to invite him to her birthday party. Tracie had asked her to do it—begged her to, really. But she didn't want to give him the wrong idea. She'd have to make it clear that she was inviting him on behalf of her friend.

If she put it in writing, she could make it very clear. She bent over her desk, covering her notebook so no one could see what she was writing. *Dear Carter,* she started.

No. That was too personal. She had to be more aloof, almost like she was Tracie's secretary.

Carter: she wrote. *Tracie is wondering whether you could go with her to my birthday party.*

She put down her pen. Writing a note to a friend's crush seemed too middle school.

"This will be on Friday's test," Ms. Viola said.

What will be on Friday's test? Crap. Sienna had totally tuned out. She stopped composing the note and listened for a while, but it was so boring.

She looked at the clock again. Twenty-six minutes left now. Could this class go any slower? She sensed Carter watching her and felt her face go warm. She fiddled with her pencil, sneaked a glance at him, listened to the teacher's drones again.

Someone handed her a note. *S, You look cute when you're distracted. C.*

Argh! Carter knew! She wondered if he also knew that he had caused her to be distracted in the first place.

Stop it, she told herself. *Carter's saved for Tracie, not you.*

Thinking about that made her face even warmer. She told herself to hurry up and ask him to the party on Tracie's behalf.

"So I hope you understand the eight poetic forms I've discussed the last few days," the teacher said.

Were there eight? Hell, she probably knew only two or three of them. Well, it was her last semester of senior year and she'd already been accepted to CalTech. She was entitled to slack off. Besides, she was so distracted. She felt his gaze on her again. She concentrated on the paper in front of her and wrote, *Carter, Tracie requested that I invite you to serve as her escort at my birthday party.*

No. That sounded too formal. She wanted to invite him in a friendly way. She also wanted something to do besides listen to Vile Viola.

She had a terrific idea. She could write to Carter in poem form. If she kept it light, he couldn't think about her seriously. That's what she told herself, anyway, as she tuned out the teacher again and started writing. *Carter, you're invited to something great. Your friend Sienna is turning ten and eight. We'll dance on a yacht to celebrate.* This poem was so silly and fun to write. She hoped he'd appreciate it. *The party is this Saturday at eight. Tracie wants you to be her date. I hope you'll come and not be late.* She smiled as she wrote it, smiled as she read it over, smiled as she folded it up, then dropped the smile as she glanced at Carter. He was staring at her again.

Before she could change her mind, she quietly asked the girl sitting next to her to pass the note to Carter.

She watched him unfold it, staring at his face as he read it. *If I were a better friend to Tracie,* she told herself, *I wouldn't care so much about Carter's expression as he read my poem. A silly poem,* she told herself, *just for laughs.* There was nothing flirtatious in it. In fact, she'd called herself *your friend Sienna* and written *Tracie wants you to be her date.* That should have set the "just friends" tone.

It was hard to figure out Carter's reaction to the note. He'd been staring at the notepaper as if she'd written a novella on it, or—what was that called?—an epic poem. He should be done by now. He didn't lift his head. His eyes remained downcast. Then he put the note aside. *Just like that?* Sienna wondered. As if it meant nothing?

"Sienna Douglas, are you paying attention to me or your classmates?" the teacher said.

Argh! Just one classmate, if Miss Viola really wanted to know. Right before she jerked her gaze from Carter, she thought she saw him smile.

Oh, very funny, she thought. *I'm feeling guilty enough about gawking at you because you're Tracie's ex, and now I have to worry it'll get me reamed out by Vile Viola too.*

The teacher started in on another type of poem with a long name that Sienna had never heard of.

Sienna sneaked a glance at Carter again. He was scribbling something furiously onto a wrinkled piece of notebook paper. *What?* She squinted, but couldn't see a thing. *What was he writing?* she wondered. Why was she so interested in Tracie's ex? That was the real question. She didn't want to answer that.

She looked away, tried to concentrate on the lesson, didn't listen to a word the teacher said, gawked at Carter again.

He passed the note to the girl next to him, who passed it to Sienna.

She made herself unfold it slowly because she was sure Carter was watching her. After she finished it, she realized she'd been smiling the whole time she read it.

She forced the smile off her face. She read the note again. The smile crept back. It remained through the third reading. She was able to keep it off as she read the note for the fourth time, and the fifth.

After that, she folded it and slipped it into her purse. She didn't have to look at it anymore because she'd memorized it. As the teacher droned on, Sienna chanted to herself, *I'll take your friend along with me, to your party out at sea. But it's really you with whom I want to be.*

She felt Carter's gaze on her, but stared at her desk for the rest of the period. If their eyes were to meet, she didn't think she'd be able to look away. She worried she couldn't keep resisting him.

As soon as the bell rang, she rushed out of her seat and out the door. It was wrong for Carter to flirt with her. And it was wrong for her to like it so much. It was horrible to steal your best friend's boyfriend.

But other thoughts, unkind ones, crept into her head. For one thing, Carter wasn't Tracie's boyfriend anymore. What if he never wanted to be again? Would it be so awful if Sienna were to hang out with him—or more?

sixteen

After school, Sienna walked down the hallway with a strong sense of purpose. Ever since English class today, Sienna knew she had to stop flirting with Carter. She and Tracie had been friends a lot longer than she'd known Carter. And Tracie and Carter had gone out for years. To risk losing her best friend for a fling with Carter was just not worth it. Besides, it wasn't right. She needed to let Carter know that she was off limits.

He was probably still at school. He was involved in so many activities—student government, Key Club, swim team—he was bound to be at some meeting or practice. She had been to the classrooms where student council and Key Club usually met, to no avail. Now she headed for the pool. She hoped to find Carter there, tell him Tracie missed him, and hopefully reunite them and make them both happy.

Then I'll be the only miserable one, she thought, *spending my weekends alone while everyone else is coupled up.*

Sienna shook her head. She wasn't going to walk around feeling sorry for herself, or refuse to help her friend find happiness.

As she approached the pool, Sienna heard the sounds of a piercing whistle, lots of splashing, and a woman's high voice shrieking, "Go, go, go!" She opened the gate. A short woman, obviously a coach, cheered on the swim team while they practiced relays in the bright blue water. They were so fast. Sienna looked for Carter, but all she could see was a blur of high arms and quick legs and heads in bathing caps bobbing through the water.

After they finished, the little coach yelled, "That was great! You're swimming like winners! If you swim like that at the next meet, I think we'll see gold. Now get out of the water, clap yourselves on your backs, and take a fifteen-minute break."

Sienna watched as the swimmers got out of the pool. She spotted Carter as he climbed a ladder and rushed out. A yard or so from the pool, he stopped and tore off his bathing cap. His thick golden hair spilled out freely like the mane of a lion king. He was a glorious sight, with his wet, muscular, hairless chest, his long, firm legs, and his Speedo—especially his Speedo—which was quite revealing, in a very good way.

"Sienna!" he called out to her, grinning.

Oh, yikes. What was she doing gawking at him like that? She was supposed to be winning back Carter for her best friend, not staring at him like he was the star of a strip show.

"Sienna?" he asked her.

You idiot, say something, she lectured herself. *And get your eyes off Carter's Speedo, you perv.* "Hey, Carter." Her voice came out squeaky. She cleared her throat and tried again. "Hey, I was looking for you."

He walked toward her. His bare chest revealed muscles she never knew he possessed.

Stop thinking like that, she scolded herself.

A couple yards away from her, he leaned down and pulled out a towel from a plastic trunk on the cement ground. He wrapped the towel around his waist and headed toward her.

She forced herself not to look at him below his neck. Or at least below his shoulders—his broad, muscular shoulders. She told herself, *Don't look at his beefy chest or long legs.* Then she stared at both of them.

"You okay? You seem a little out of it," Carter said.

"I'm great." She knew she was blushing. Her cheeks felt like hot cherry pie.

"You came to see me?"

She cleared her throat again. "On behalf of Tracie."

"Oh." He seemed less than enthusiastic. "How is she doing?"

"She misses you."

He shrugged.

"Tracie made mistakes. She's really sorry."

"It's okay. What's done is done," Carter said.

"It can be undone," Sienna suggested. "You guys haven't been broken up that long."

"I don't want to get back together with her," he said. "There's someone else I'm interested in."

"I . . . I've got to go," Sienna managed to stammer. "I've got, um, homework and stuff."

Carter nodded. "Right. Homework and stuff. Probably a bad idea for us to go somewhere by ourselves, huh?"

"Yeah," Sienna said. "And your swim coach . . ." Had he always had all those muscles? When had his shoulders gotten so broad? *Stop it, Sienna. You have to stay away. Even if he's not interested in Tracie. Even if he likes you. Even if he has the most amazing body you've ever seen. You can't do this to your best friend.*

"Sienna? Why did you really come to see me today?" he asked.

"For Tracie. Because she's my friend." That's what she had told herself, anyway, as she searched all over school for him. "I need to go. I have . . ."

"Homework and stuff?" Carter smirked at her.

"Right. Homework. And stuff. So . . . So, good-bye."

"Bye, Sienna. Thanks a lot for coming by to see me."

She rushed away. The gate leading from the swimming pool was jammed. She couldn't push it open.

"You have to pull it!" Carter called out.

Oh, hell. Now her cheeks were so hot, she wouldn't have been surprised if her face burned off. She pulled on the door and made her escape.

seventeen

"I hope people come to this," Mark said as he and the rest of the band set up their instruments outside the entrance to Macy's. He was more worried than he let on to his band-mates. How many people went to the mall on a Wednesday night? Of those who did, how many would take time out from shopping to listen to an unknown band? He figured the number to be in the single digits.

"I hope we get an audience too," Sienna said as she tuned her guitar. "Tracie, I love that dried flower you put in your hair. The peach color goes so well with the blond color."

"Thanks," Tracie said.

Lily sidled up to Mark and he put his arm around her. She squeezed in closer to him. "I'm freezing."

"It's your fault for wearing a miniskirt and tiny T-shirt," Sienna said with a snide tone.

"Come on, everyone," Mark begged. "We're going to perform at the mall. This should be fun."

"I love performing and I love the mall," Tracie said. "Performing at the mall? There's nothing better."

"Unless the Chargers cheerleaders show up and cheer us on. Or maybe a few Victoria's Secret models," George said. "Now that would beat the performance/mall combo."

Sienna laughed. "They probably have better things to do. Like feed their goldfish. It looks like everyone has something better to do. There's barely anyone here."

"I put the gig on the front page of our website," George said, "but we still aren't getting that many hits on the site."

"Guyda told me that once we start playing, we'll draw a crowd," Mark said. "He said he really had to schmooze the manager here to let us perform. He tried his best. Now let's try our best."

Next to him, Lily tossed her hair. "Is Guyda working for us, or are we working for him? You're always defending him."

"I just don't want us to have a defeatist attitude before we even start playing," Mark said.

Lily inched away from him. One of the things he loved about her was her tough spirit and strong will. But sometimes, like today, it made for disquieting conflict between them.

"Well, let's just play our music and see who comes," Mark said. "Even if we don't get an audience, we can treat this like a rehearsal. We could use one. We only have three days until we perform at The Spot. Let's start with 'School Bites After Being Out All Night.' Three, two, one. Rock!"

George started drumming, then Sienna and Tracie joined in on their guitars, and Mark added piano music tweaked with synthesized French horn. It was a fun song, though it was weird to play it in an empty mall.

A couple of women laden with shopping bags stopped in front of the band. Then a guy in a Harley-Davidson jacket, holding the hand of a girl covered with tattoos, came by and they both tapped their feet to the music.

By the time they'd finished that song and started "Touch Me, Thrill Me," a crowd had gathered, small but attentive. There was a middle-aged woman wearing a Macy's badge, probably just leaving work, a woman with an infant in a stroller, about ten teenagers, a few preteens, and even two elderly women who were swaying to the music.

"Thanks for stopping and listening," Sienna said to their small audience. She walked over to them and handed out flyers promoting Amber Road's MySpace page and website, as well as their Saturday night gig at The Spot.

Mark called out to the audience, "You feel like a love song or a party song next?" Most of the guys called out for a party song, while the girls wanted a love song. "Typical, typical," Mark joked. He loved this interaction. Up to now, they'd mostly been onstage in the dark, just playing their music without talking to the crowd.

"Mark, you need to write a love song with partying," Lily joked.

"No. A party song with a little love thrown in," George said.

"If you stay, we'll play both," Mark said. "I think some of these guys will like 'Rock It Like a Rocket,' and you beautiful girls," he gestured to the audience, "might like 'Beautiful Girl,' which we actually just recorded a few days ago."

They played the songs to cheers and whistles and hollers, and a growing crowd. Lily tossed keychains into the audience, and Mark loved seeing people dive for them like they were home-run balls at a Padres game.

While they were joking with the audience, Steve Guyda came by, sipping a large cup of coffee. He put his arm over Mark's shoulder and shouted, "Are these kids hot or what? They're going places, and soon you're going to be bragging to your friends you knew them when."

"Aw, shucks," George said.

"Anyone here like to surf?" Guyda shouted.

Some of the teenagers clapped and the Macy's employee shouted, "Every chance I can get!"

"Did you hear Amber Road's cover of the song 'Surf's Up'?" Guyda asked the crowd.

"No-o-o," they shouted.

"I think they do it even better than Daybreak did. Play it, guys. Then go straight into 'I'm So into You, I Don't Know What to Do.'"

Mark glanced at Lily. She shook her head.

"Let's hear them!" one of the teenagers in the audience shouted.

Mark turned away from Lily, planted a smile on, and yelled with fake enthusiasm, "Three, two, one. Rock!"

Everyone in the audience stayed for both songs, and about ten new people joined them. They clapped afterward, but nobody shouted or yelled "More!" like they did before. Mark wasn't sure whether it was because the new songs weren't very good or because the band's lack of enthusiasm showed.

"They'll take a five-minute break," Guyda said.

"We will?" Lily said.

Mark was thinking the same thing. Who was Guyda to tell them when they should take a break? But he hadn't dared say it. "Come on, guys, I'm kind of tired anyway," Mark said.

They huddled behind their instruments. "I think we should be the ones deciding when to take a break," Sienna muttered.

Mark tried to look on the bright side. *For once Sienna and Lily actually agree on something,* he told himself.

Guyda either hadn't heard their complaints or ignored them. "Did you advertise this performance on your website?" he asked.

"We did," George said. "Right on the front page."

"How many hits are you getting?"

"Not a lot," George mumbled.

"Not enough, obviously. You need to work on getting your name out. On the Net and around town too." Guyda took a big gulp of coffee. "I put up that great MySpace page for Amber Road, but you kids have to help lead people to it. I've said it before and I'll say it again: it's not just about talent. It's about promotion and persistence. Don't waste my time if you're not going to make the effort."

"Sorry. We'll try harder," Mark said, suspecting that Lily was going to call him an apologist or a wimp later.

"You guys made a set list, right?" Guyda asked.

Mark shrugged. "We thought we'd just see how it goes, what the crowd is like."

Guyda shook his head. "You need a set list every time, and from now on I'd like to approve it first. You have to act like professionals and listen to your manager."

"Fine," Mark said. "Who's got a pen and paper?"

Guyda reached into his briefcase and pulled out both. "I'll make the set list for you. This is a good chance to try out some more of those songs I gave you. Perfect for the mall crowd."

"But is the mall crowd perfect for us?" George asked as an elderly woman with a walker ambled past them.

Guyda said. "If not, I have a plan to get a better crowd." He handed Mark the paper. "Here's your set list."

Mark stared at the paper. "But none of these are our songs. We didn't write a single one of them."

"So make them your own," Guyda said. "Now let's hear your sound."

Daybreak's sound, actually, Mark thought. But he said, "Come on, guys," and led his friends back to their instruments. Standing over the keyboard, he said, "Next up is 'Shop 'Til You Drop.' "

Beside him, Lily softly said, "Ugh."

"One, two, three. Rock!" Mark shouted with fake enthusiasm. They sang the song. It wasn't bad, and a song about shopping was appropriate for the mall. But it wasn't great either. Their audience slowly dissipated. A few new people came, but most didn't stay long. Mark was grateful when the song ended.

"Hey, Brandon!" Tracie called out. The bartender at Waves was walking toward them. "What are you doing here?" she asked.

He stopped in front of them. "I came by to listen to you, of course. I like the rose in your hair," he told Tracie.

"You actually went to our website and read that we were playing?" George asked.

Brandon laughed. "Yeah. Is that a problem?"

"Not at all, dude. Welcome," George said.

"You guys still playing?" Brandon asked.

"I guess," Mark looked down at the set list Guyda had scribbled for him. "Next is 'Sweet As Sugar,'" he announced while trying not to grimace.

"Hold on. One more short break," Guyda said.

Lily sighed loudly. Mark sighed quietly. Still, they huddled with Guyda behind their instruments.

"I want a couple of you to go through the mall, singing and handing out flyers and letting everyone know the show will start in fifteen minutes," their manager said. "Sienna and Lily, you're both pretty. You both have the voices. Go ahead."

Uh-oh. Mark suspected Lily wouldn't exactly be jumping at the opportunity. He glanced at her.

He was right. Her arms were crossed. "You want me and Sienna to hustle the shoppers at the mall?" she asked with a sneer.

"That's way too tacky," Sienna said.

"Do you want to be a success or not?" Guyda said.

"Not that badly," Lily said.

"I'll go with you," Mark said. "I can sing too."

Lily threw her arms up in an exaggerated sign of defeat. "Fine."

"I'll stay out here," Sienna said, sounding relieved.

Mark and Lily took a bunch of flyers and began to make their way through the mall. "You know I wouldn't do this for anyone but you," Lily told him.

"I appreciate it." Mark put his arm around her again as they walked. "Thanks for being there for me. For us. Let's try to bring in a huge crowd."

They didn't have much luck. They got jeered at by a foursome of middle-school goth kids, had their cheeks pinched by an old man who smelled like mothballs, were ignored by hundreds of shoppers, and met maybe six or eight people who said they'd go listen to Amber Road.

He and Lily headed back with most of their flyers in hand. They joined the others and played a few mediocre songs from Guyda's set list. There were about fifteen people in the audience, nowhere near the size of the crowd they had when they played their own stuff.

Guyda finally said, "Let's call it a night."

None of the band members objected.

Mark drove Lily home. They didn't talk much. He knew she was upset. Every time he caught a glimpse of her in the passenger seat, she was pouting or shaking her head.

He didn't want her to leave angry. At least they should talk about their lousy night, even though Mark knew it wouldn't be a pleasant conversation. He decided to make light of the situation. "The songs Guyda gave us are about as exciting as mashed potatoes."

"You said it." Lily frowned.

"I was kind of joking," Mark said. "Hey, at least that bartender, Brandon, seemed to like us."

"Whoopee," she muttered.

"I'm sorry. I know you're mad."

"Me? Mad?" Lily asked. "Just because I spent the last hour playing cornball songs, and getting dissed by a bunch of mall-rats, including some middle-school cretins I never would have talked to if you and our slavemaster Guyda hadn't made me."

"Oh, Lily. Can you look on the bright side at all?" Mark asked as he turned down her street. "Things can only get better."

"No. The way I see it, things can only get worse. Ever since we signed on with Steve Guyda, we've been losing a little more of our identity every day. Can you imagine us playing songs like that before Guyda got here? And begging people to come and listen to us for free?"

"Hey, Guyda's gotten us plenty of paying gigs too." Mark parked in front of her house. "We wouldn't be performing at The Spot without him managing us."

"I don't want to be performing someone else's songs. We should be doing our own. We should fire our manager and go back to making our own decisions," Lily said as she unbuckled her seat belt.

"I don't want to do that. Not when we have all this momentum."

"I knew you'd say that." Lily opened the car door.

"Lily, I don't want you to leave when you're upset." Mark's voice was choked. "How about we go out for a late dinner? I'll take you wherever you want to go. Italian at the Gaslamp? Or there's a new sushi place in Hillcrest that's supposed to be good. Anywhere." He knew he must sound pathetic, but it was killing him that she was so angry. He'd much rather give up his pride than his girlfriend. "And we won't talk about band stuff at all," he continued. "I could spend the evening talking about how much I love you."

"Oh, Mark." She smiled. "You know I love you too. I just . . . Playing those lame cover songs and then trying to pimp our stupid band. Ugh. I just need time to cool off."

"Let's cool off together," Mark said. "We could go for a dip in the Jacuzzi again, just the two of us. Though I bet that'll make me hot instead." He winked at her, comically.

She laughed. "It sounds really tempting. But I promised Aaron I'd be home for dinner. He's giving me a lot of crap about not being around anymore. I can't keep blowing him off."

"I understand," Mark said, although he didn't. "Sorry about today." He reached over and kissed her before she got out of the car, and things felt all right again. Almost.

eighteen

It was the night of the party—and Tracie's date with Carter. Finally. Tracie was so excited she was pacing her bedroom. This was it. This was her chance to reunite with Carter and be happy again.

The doorbell rang at 6:30 sharp. Carter was exactly on time. His reliability was something she'd always liked about him. Though, come to think of it, when they'd dated she had complained he was *too* reliable. That was dumb of her. She'd wound up with Aaron instead, who could be a half-hour late and shrug it off as no big deal. She'd learned her lesson. She'd pick reliable over irresponsible any day.

Tracie didn't rush to meet Carter at the door. She didn't want to reveal how eager she was to go out with him again. Besides, she wanted to see herself in her mirror once more.

Sometimes she hated how she looked—too pale, too thin, too flat. But tonight was not one of those times. The dress she and Sienna had found at the mall was perfect—a long turquoise sheath, which somehow made every part of her look better. It made her skin appear softer and her eyes appear brighter. The dangling crystal earrings borrowed from her mother added more sparkle, and her new black stilettos made her legs appear long; even her feet looked sexy. And she was lucky enough tonight not to have any blemishes. She smiled at the mirror as her mother called, "Carter's here!"

She walked out to greet him. He stood between her parents in a shiny tuxedo, which he wore well. "It's so good to see you, dear," her mother told Carter. "It's been a long time. Much too long." It seemed as if her parents had missed Carter as much as she had. Her mother positively glowed. "Carter, you look super tonight," she said.

Super? Had anyone used that word after 1955? At least her mother hadn't told Carter he looked neato or keen.

But Carter's grin was not a mocking one. And when he said, "It's good to see you too, Dr. and Mrs. Grant," he sounded sincere.

"And how about our beautiful daughter?" her mother said. "Isn't Tracie just stunning?"

"I believe you need a cover-up around you," her father grumbled. Could they embarrass her any further?

"Our Tracie's not a little girl anymore, that's for sure," her mother said. Yes, they could embarrass her further. God!

Carter didn't remark on her appearance. *Maybe*, Tracie thought, *he's waiting until we're alone.* He was nice, though, otherwise. He even let Tracie's parents take pictures—lots and lots and lots of pictures.

While Carter had his arm around her for the camera, Tracie imagined it was just like old times, when she felt safe and happy. It wasn't like being with Aaron, not exciting like that. But Aaron had hurt her, and Carter never had.

"What have you been up to, son?" Tracie's father asked Carter. "We haven't seen you in a good month or so."

Carter's cheeks got rosy. "Oh, you know. I've been busy. Lots of stuff going on."

"That's okay, dear," her mother said. "We know how it is. Tracie's been so busy herself, working terribly hard on a report at the library, and sleeping over at her new friend Lily's house. I'm glad you two are going to Sienna's party tonight."

Oh, God. She hadn't been to the library in ages and hadn't really befriended Lily either. Those were just her old alibis. When she and Aaron had been messing around, they told her parents they were study partners who spent a lot of time at the library. And she used to tell them she was spending the night at Lily's house, which was only technically true. She'd slept over Lily's house, but in Aaron's bedroom. "We'd better get going," Tracie mumbled.

They watched Carter and her the entire time they were leaving—out the front door, down the steps, through the driveway, and into Carter's car as he held open her door. They waved good-bye as Carter drove off. Tracie was relieved to get out of there. And she was overjoyed to be with Carter again. Not *with* him with him, but next to him in his Prius again. She owed Sienna big time for setting this up.

"You told your folks you were going to the library? And to Lily's house?" Carter asked at the stop sign by her house.

"It was stupid of me." The less said about her going out with Aaron the better. She knew she'd hurt Carter badly then. What a mistake she had made. "Can we just forget the last month? I was an idiot, okay?" she said.

Carter didn't answer.

"How's swimming going?" she asked him. "I read in the paper that you set a school record. Congratulations."

"Thanks. It's been a rush, but also kind of a bummer because it's my last year competing for the high school. I've made some good friends, being on the team for four years."

"We were together a long time," Tracie reminded him.

He nodded. "Did you finish your history essay?"

"I'm almost done with it." History essay? He was making small talk, acting like they were acquaintances rather than two people who had dated for most of high school. She wouldn't let him go without a fight. "I'm not going out with anyone, you know," she said.

He didn't respond.

"Are you seeing anyone?" she asked.

He shook his head.

They were silent for a while—an agonizing while. *I guess he's not going to say anything about my dress,* Tracie told herself. *I wonder if he even noticed it, being so preoccupied with avoiding real conversation.* "So have you been looking forward to tonight?" she asked him.

"I bet the food will be good."

"What?"

"The food. At Sienna's party tonight."

God, he refused to talk about anything of substance. Well, she would. "It feels weird not to be dating you. We were together for such a long time."

"People change," he said. "I understand that."

What did he mean? Did he think she had changed so much she wasn't interested in him anymore? He was wrong. It was true that she had changed. But she hadn't changed so much that she didn't want Carter back in her life again. "People make mistakes," she told him. "I've made mistakes."

"We're here." He drove into the entrance to the harbor. It was clear to Tracie that it would be hard to get him to open up. He found a parking spot, stopped the car, and rushed out. He hurried to her side and opened the door for her.

God, she had missed that. She had always taken his politeness for granted. She thanked him, but he was already a few feet ahead of her, rushing to the yacht.

The boat was really pretty, glowing over the water with hundreds of tiny white lights around its railing. Throughout the yacht, pale balloons were grouped in big displays, spelling out Sienna and eighteen and forming large, beautiful hearts. This party was going to be lavish and lush. Sienna's mother was a dot-com millionaire, and not only had money to burn but great taste too.

If only the car ride with Carter had gone differently, the romantic setting would have been perfect for rekindling their romance. But Carter acted as if reuniting was the furthest thing from his mind. "What a great party," he said. "I'm glad Sienna invited me. She's got great taste in music."

"I helped her pick out that band," Tracie said. Yes, this was Sienna's big night, but couldn't Carter pay a little attention to her too? This *was* supposed to be a date, after all.

The steel drum band *was* excellent. A few couples, including Sienna's parents, were already on the dance floor. Dozens of people, beautifully dressed, stood on the boat. Lily and Mark were there, holding hands at the edge of the dance floor and swaying to the music.

Carter hurried over to them, as if he hated to be alone with Tracie. She didn't know if he was mad at her or just completely over her. She hoped it was the former. At least it would show he had some kind of feelings toward her.

She stayed where she was, near the entrance to the boat. Carter didn't even turn around or pause to look for her. A slim man in a white tuxedo offered her a lobster roll from the silver tray he carried. Tracie turned it down. She'd lost her appetite.

George tapped her on the shoulder. "Next time someone offers you those lobster things, grab a handful of them and give them to me. I had six of them already, plus half a tray of bacon and scallops and about half a pound of meatballs. The waiters are now avoiding me like Brussels sprouts."

"Maybe it's the dog," Tracie said. Next to George, a scrawny girl in a tight, lace blouse and giant hoopskirt held a Chihuahua in her arms.

"Everyone loves Pupcakes!" the girl exclaimed. She kissed it unnervingly close to its mouth.

"Tracie, meet Becca, my date," George said.

"And this is my dog, Pupcakes," Becca said. "Isn't she the sweetest?"

Tracie put her hand out to pat Pupcakes, but the dog growled at her.

"You're looking great tonight, Tracie," George told her.

At least someone thinks so, she said to herself.

He took Becca's hand. "I'm lucky to be standing between the two prettiest girls in California."

The dog let out a series of loud yaps.

"Pupcakes is a girl too, you know," Becca shouted over her dog.

"Hey, what about me? I'm not in your top three?" Sienna pushed George's shoulder playfully.

"Oops. You too," he said. "And Lily. And anyone else within earshot."

Tracie hugged Sienna. "Happy birthday! You look beautiful." She did. She wore a long white, strapless dress that clung to her curves and showed off her bright white smile. Her hair was swept up, giving her added height and elegance, and her thick red lipstick and ruby necklace added drama to her appearance.

"Oh, I just happened to have this outfit in my closet, and I threw my hair in a bun to get it out of my eyes," Sienna said.

Tracie winked at her. "Of course." She knew Sienna had spent close to five hundred dollars on her dress and shoes, and had been at the beauty salon most of the afternoon.

"You really know how to throw a party!" George said.

Sienna beamed. "I'm already having so much fun, and we're only just leaving the dock now." She turned back to

Tracie. "You look divine, girl. Where's your date? Did he faint at the mere sight of you?"

"Ha, ha. Not exactly," Tracie said. She didn't want to burden Sienna with her troubles on Sienna's birthday. So she simply said, "I just saw Carter a few minutes ago. I'm sure he'll be back soon."

"Hey, birthday girl." Carter came up behind them and hugged Sienna. "You are one terrific-looking eighteen-year-old."

Sienna's smile grew even bigger. "Thanks. You're sweet."

"I'm not just being sweet," Carter said. "You really do look terrific. Of course, you always look terrific. But in that dress you seem even more so, like a princess."

Tracie couldn't believe it. He hadn't said one nice thing about her the entire way over, and now he couldn't stop complimenting Sienna. Was he just being sweet to her because it was her birthday? But shouldn't he be sweet to his date too?

She needed a drink. She grabbed Carter's hand. "Let's go order something at the bar. I'm thirsty."

He shrugged and let her lead him away. They walked past the near-empty dance floor to the crowded bar. She knew with Sienna's parents and family friends on the boat, they wouldn't serve her alcohol. But she had come prepared.

"You want a Diet Coke?" Carter asked her as he got near the front of the drink line.

"Yeah, I haven't changed that much." She'd been ordering Diet Coke for years. Of course, now she preferred a real drink, but Carter didn't have to know that.

He handed her the glass of soda. She thanked him and took a sip before telling him she'd be back in a minute. Then she rushed off, stood against the side of the boat, and quietly slipped a small water bottle half filled with rum out of her purse. She'd gotten the idea from Aaron. He used to sneak liquor into movie theaters that way. The bottle of rum had been sitting in her parents' pantry for years, three-quarters full. Now it was half full. Her parents would never notice. *It's not like I need alcohol*, Tracie told herself. *It's just that tonight is important and I want to be able to relax, to have fun, to party!*

By the time she got back to Carter, she'd gulped down half her drink. Fortified by the liquor, she moved close to him and said, "It's great to be here with you."

"What were you doing?" Carter asked her.

"Nothing."

Carter shook his head. "I'm not a partier like Aaron Bouchet, but I can smell alcohol on people's breath. I can't believe you brought liquor to your best friend's birthday party, with her parents right here."

"They won't find out," Tracie muttered, "unless someone tells them."

"Can't you have fun without drinking anymore?" He shook his head. "I don't even know who you are now."

She was a lonely girl who hated being the object of Carter's loathing, that's who. "Carter please. I was just . . ." *Just drinking to forget how miserable I am.* She couldn't say that though. "I was just experimenting. It was stupid. I won't even take another sip, okay?"

"Do whatever you want. We're not going out anymore," he said coldly.

"But we could," Tracie pleaded. "What's stopping us?"

He shook his head.

"I haven't changed that much," Tracie said. "I'm really the same old me." But that was a lie. Before she had been happy. She and Carter had trusted each other, and she hadn't been humiliated by Aaron Bouchet. She hadn't been drinking almost every night. She hadn't felt so completely alone, as if nobody cared about her or wanted to be with her. Carter used to care about her so much.

She bit her lip. The only thing to do was to keep trying to get him back. And maybe also drink more of her rum.

nineteen

Sienna stood at the railing, watching the yacht set sail on the Pacific Ocean. It was beautiful outside tonight, with hundreds of boats of all sizes and types moored to the dock, the stars sparkling under a sliver of moon, the waves gently lapping underneath her, birds swooping by and calling out to each other every so often.

Sienna turned around and studied her guests on deck. Almost everyone she'd invited had been able to come. The girls looked fantastic in their glittery makeup, soft dresses, and delicate, high-heeled shoes. The boys mostly seemed uncomfortable, fingering their ties and moving slowly in their bulky suits and shiny tuxedos and heavy dress shoes. Still, they flirted and laughed and some of them kissed, and they ate the seemingly endless supply of fancy hors d'oeuvres handed out by the straight-faced catering staff.

She'd been looking forward to this party for ages, and it was exceeding her expectations. She gazed at her parents, holding hands as they sauntered around the deck making sure everyone was content. *They won't have much work to do on that front*, Sienna thought. Even Tracie must feel happy tonight, finally.

She watched Tracie and Carter once again. They were still at the bar. She had never seen Carter in a tuxedo before. He looked so handsome, like a leading man at a Hollywood awards show. And Tracie had never looked better. It was as if that dress had been designed and sewn just for her. Everything about it—the color, the cut, the fit—was perfect.

The beautiful couple, Tracie and Carter, wouldn't even be together tonight if not for her. Maybe in a few years they'd get married, and she would be Tracie's maid of honor, and Tracie would thank her in her speech at the reception. She tried to tell herself she'd done the right thing inviting Carter as Tracie's date. He was a good guy, and she knew he'd take good care of Tracie.

After seeing Tracie in her gorgeous dress, talking with her alone in his car and on this romantic yacht, under the clear night sky with a light breeze, Carter would probably fall in love with Tracie all over again. He and Tracie had been standing together at the bar for a long time, barely talking to anyone else, including Sienna. Maybe they had already reunited. *Wonderful,* she told herself. *It's just what your best friend needs and wants.* She should be so happy for the two of them. She should. Unfortunately, knowing how she should feel and actually feeling that way were two different things.

Sienna turned away from Carter and Tracie. It was her birthday—*her* night. Lately she had spent so much time and effort worrying about Tracie. Tonight, for a change, she would enjoy being the center of attention. And so far, she really had. So many people had complimented her tonight, calling her pretty and lovely and beautiful, and saying she looked just like a young Halle Berry. Carter had called her a princess, and said she looked terrific. She realized, with a measure of guilt, that his compliments meant more to her than anyone's.

Her father walked toward her. She duplicated his broad smile. She wasn't used to him appearing so dapper. As a math professor at UC San Diego, he usually was more interested in writing voluminous proofs of complex theorems than buying new clothes. But he had listened to Sienna's mother and bought a tuxedo. The glossy black jacket added just the right shading to his soft black complexion. He had even gone to an expensive hairdresser today instead of the barber in National City he usually frequented. Sienna thought she actually noticed hair product—mousse or gel—in his thinning, salt-and-pepper hair.

He kissed her on the cheek. "Happy birthday, darling. You doing all right?"

Her smile grew. "I've never been better. Thank you so much for throwing this party."

"Your mother did all the legwork. I just paid for it. Come to think of it, your mother did that too."

Sienna laughed. "Well, I really appreciate you getting all spiffed up for this."

"That was the hardest part." He laughed. "I miss my sneakers and old corduroy slacks. As long as I'm all gussied up, and have the privilege of talking to you alone for a change without your friends swarming around you, I'd love a dance with you."

"Oh, Daddy, that would be great."

They walked to the dance floor with his arm around her. *Thank God a slow song is playing*, she thought. She'd seen her father boogie last year at her cousin Rayshawnda's wedding—not a pretty sight.

Her face tensed up as she approached the dance floor. There were a few couples on it, but two people attracted her attention. Carter and Tracie swayed to the music with their arms wrapped around each other. Would Carter ever dance with her like that? Sienna pushed the thought out of her mind. Next to them, dancing about as close as two people physically could without having sex, were Mark and Lily.

"You okay, sweetheart?" her father asked.

She turned her focus back to him, or tried to, at least. "I'm great, Daddy."

Her father put his sturdy arms around her. As they danced, Sienna reminded herself how lucky she was. She had great parents, for one thing. She shouldn't be jealous of Lily, even though Lily was beautiful and had a wonderful singing voice and was breathing in Mark's ear right now. Even though Lily had stolen Mark from her. Lily's life was far from perfect. She had her horrible twin brother, Aaron, to contend with. And

Sienna suspected that Lily and Aaron's parents neglected them. It seemed like they were always out of town.

The song ended, and she hugged her father and thanked him for the dance.

"I'm honored you agreed to share your first dance tonight with your old man," he said. "But I don't want to keep you from your friends."

"May I have the honor of a dance?" Carter asked.

Her mouth dropped open. She looked at Tracie, who remained on the dance floor where she'd just been with Carter. Now Tracie's eyes were no longer sparkling; they were burning. Her lips, colored with pink lipstick and darker pink lip liner borrowed from Sienna, were pursed as she stared at Sienna and Carter. Sienna knew her friend well enough to have a pretty good idea what she was thinking. *How dare Carter and Sienna dance together.*

Sienna frowned. It wasn't her fault Carter wanted to dance with her. She hadn't even been watching him most of the time she was on the dance floor. But she suspected Tracie would make up some sort of conspiracy theory and blame them both. Well, Tracie's insecurities wouldn't stop her from dancing with a friend on her birthday. "Thank you," she told Carter. "I'd love to dance."

He wrapped his arms around her. They were warm and strong and felt just right against her back. His hands settled a little above her bottom. She stopped thinking of Tracie. She stopped thinking of anything except how he felt against her— very good, very, very good. She felt engulfed by passion. She closed her eyes, and when Carter leaned into her, she moved even closer to him. There was that aroma of his again—like spiced apple cider. She drank him in.

No! This was so wrong. Carter had just danced with Tracie. He was supposed to be Tracie's date. And Sienna was supposed to be Tracie's best friend.

"You're a great dancer," Carter murmured. "And you fit just right in my arms, like we were made for each other."

She dug her nails into her palm. "Tracie and I used to practice together in sixth grade. You should have seen us. We took turns over who had to take the guy's part." She would keep reminding him of Tracie, of her relationship with her. She would not dishonor her best friend. She would not be controlled by passion.

But again, there was that difference between how she *should* feel and how she actually felt. She felt good in his arms, as if she belonged there, no matter how much she told herself she didn't. If he weren't Tracie's ex-boyfriend, if Tracie hadn't wanted him back, if she weren't a loyal friend . . . But she had to face reality. She could not have Carter. It just wasn't right. No matter how right it felt.

When the song ended, she didn't look Tracie's way, but she still sensed Tracie glaring at her with fiery eyes.

"One more dance?" Carter whispered in her ear.

"I . . ." She wanted so much to say yes. "Don't you need to get back to Tracie?"

"I suppose so." But he drew her closer to him and she could hardly breathe, let alone object. When she did breathe, it was to savor the sweet, warm smell of him. They danced again, and it was as if they were meant to dance together, as if the entire birthday party and arranged date and maybe even their entire lives were set up just so they could get to these moments of holding each other tight and swaying to the music and realizing perfection.

When the music stopped, she made herself back up a bit from Carter's embrace and look in Tracie's direction. But Tracie was gone. If it were anyone else, she'd hardly worry. But Tracie was so emotional. Last time Tracie had seen Carter hugging her—just as friends, though the hug felt very right then too—she'd driven to the ocean and nearly drowned herself. What if Tracie did something crazy like that tonight?

Sienna wondered whether Carter was concerned too. He didn't seem to be. His eyes sparkled, warm and happy. His palms were firmly planted on her back and his shoulders leaned into hers, as if he were dancing with her in slow motion.

But they shouldn't be dancing. There wasn't even any music because the band was on a break. "We need to find Tracie," Sienna told him. "I'm worried about her."

"Oh, Sienna," Carter said. "When are you going to stop worrying about Tracie all the time and start taking care of yourself?"

"She's my best friend. I have to help her." She saw Carter's point though. She wondered if Tracie thought about her feelings even one-tenth as much as she worried about Tracie's.

But she wasn't about to turn her back on her best friend now. She scrutinized the dance floor, hoping to catch sight of her. George and his date, Becca, stood nearby, the dog in Becca's arms still. About four yards away, Lily and Mark were slow-dancing without music. Lily's body was practically glued to Mark's torso.

A few weeks ago, Sienna would have been incredibly hurt, and rightfully so. *It's totally tacky*, she thought, *to make out with a new girlfriend at your ex-girlfriend's birthday party*. But now she had come to realize that Lily and Mark had something special, something she and Mark never had, something that made them want to hold each other close like that all the time—the way Carter was holding her right now, in fact.

"We can't be standing here like this," she told Carter, "in front of everyone."

He didn't let go. "Everyone? You mean Tracie, right? And she's not here," he said.

"She should be. She came as your date." Sienna made herself back away from him and his strong but tender arms. "She must be upset. I'd better go look for her."

"At your own birthday party? That's how you want to spend your evening?" Carter shook his head.

"She's my best friend." Sienna sighed. She didn't want to be involved in Tracie's drama tonight. She felt she deserved one evening in which she, Sienna, was the center of attention for a change. But Sienna had to search for her. If she didn't, she'd be too anxious about her best friend to enjoy her party anyway. "I'm just going to make sure she's okay," she told Carter. She began pushing her way through the crowd on the dance floor.

"I'll go with you," Carter called out behind her.

As they walked through the dance floor, Sienna looked from side to side for Tracie. Now that Sienna was no longer dancing or in Carter's warm embrace, she felt cold in the windy night air. She wrapped her cashmere shawl around herself, wishing it were Carter's arms around her instead. There weren't many people left up here, and they were scattered throughout the deck. With the dark sky and the dim lighting it was hard to tell who people were, and whether Tracie was among them. The moonlight shed some of its glow onboard the yacht, but the black sky dominated. Sienna had never seen so many stars before. She felt captivated by the sight. "The moon and the stars look so bright against the dark sky," she said, staring at them.

"It's beautiful, and so are you," Carter whispered, close to her ear.

She would not let herself be romanced by Carter. They were supposed to be looking for Tracie, not starting up a relationship. She shivered, partly from the chilly temperature, but mostly out of fear about where she and Carter were headed. *This is not right,* she lectured herself again.

"Are you cold, Sienna? You're shaking." His voice was so sweet.

"Cold and scared." And excited too, though she didn't say this. She looked into his glistening eyes.

"Let me warm you," he said. Before she could protest, Carter put his long swimmer's arms around her.

She tried to make herself think about the morality of the situation. But the only thing going through her mind was how incredible his arms felt around her. And then, without thinking at all, she tilted her head to meet his, and they kissed for a long, wonderful time.

twenty

When Mark and Lily had started dancing, there were
only a few people on the dance floor. But with every new
song, it got more crowded. Now, as the band started playing
an old James Brown song, the dance floor really filled up.
Mark glanced at George and his date, still holding the Chihuahua. They were wiggling their hips and laughing. Beyond
them, Sienna's father danced jerkily as her mother, wearing a
wan smile, kept her distance.

Mark felt Lily's soft arms around his neck. She drew him
in, shaking her hips and mouthing the words of the song and
staring at Mark with her sexy blue eyes. He gladly stopped
looking at anyone else.

The song ended, but Mark didn't let go of Lily. He didn't
ever want to let her go. He kissed her and she responded

eagerly, reaching up and pressing her hands to the back of his head. Her mouth felt so good, as tender and sexy as everything else about her—her sweet scent, her willowy body, her thick, wavy hair.

After the long kiss, Mark slid his fingertip along her cheek, feeling her smooth skin, reveling in the amazing certainty that she was his. "You know I love you," he murmured, "but you probably can't imagine how *much* I love you. I don't even think there's an adequate word for what I feel."

She took his finger from her cheek and kissed it, then said, "You know I love you too. I'm crazy for you."

He closed his eyes and nodded. If only he could stay in this moment forever. They were so great together. He shouldn't have allowed himself to doubt their relationship after they had fought last week. "Lily, you make me so happy," he told her. "When you were angry with me about the songs Guyda wants us to play—"

Lily put her hand over Mark's mouth. "Shh. We're not discussing Guyda tonight. Or the songs from Daybreak. Or the band. Not even our gig at The Spot tomorrow night. No business, just pleasure."

Mark moved her hand to his chest. "I won't turn down a night of pleasure."

"Do you know what I'd like to do with you tonight?" she whispered.

He raised his eyebrows. He had some hopeful wishes.

She slowly whispered her ideas in his ear, and some of them surpassed even his most hopeful wishes.

They danced again, slowly and closely, though the band played a fast-paced song.

After many more songs, the band took a break, and Mark and Lily left the dance floor hand in hand. They walked around the yacht, stopping every so often for a drink or another kiss or to talk with a friend from school. When they got near the bow of the boat, they stood against the railing, listening to the vast roaring ocean. Mark felt awed by its endlessness and by the occasion to be alone with Lily under the moonlit sky.

He held out his arms and she fell into them. The band had started playing again. They could just make out the song from where they stood. "Shall we?" Mark asked Lily.

"Let's," she said, and they danced near the railing. While they swayed to the music, they sang together and teased each other and laughed, and said they loved each other over and over.

twenty-one

Sienna and Carter had been kissing for a long, glorious time when Sienna thought she heard footsteps coming their way, and then throat clearing and shuffling noises. But she didn't care. All she was interested in was Carter—his warm arms making her feel cared for, his strong but soft tongue urgent inside her mouth, his hands pressed against her back, though she craved them all over her body.

Then that yappy dog barked.

Damn! Sienna thought.

"Sorry for interrupting you," George said from behind her.

She and Carter pulled apart. George had his arm around his date, who had her arm around her Chihuahua. George looked down as if he was embarrassed about what he had seen. Becca peered off in the distance as if she didn't want to get involved. Well, Sienna wasn't embarrassed. Happiness was nothing to be ashamed about.

"I . . ." George started.

She wished he'd hurry up and say whatever it was he found so important. Nothing could be as important as kissing Carter right now.

"I thought you needed to know," George said.

The dog yapped.

George cleared his throat. "Uh . . ."

"Yes?" *Get on with it, already!* she wanted to shout.

"Well, Becca, my date, saw Tracie in the bathroom. She was really drunk, and looked really upset."

"Again?" Sienna asked.

"Yeah. Like when she got so drunk that night we sneaked into the Jacuzzi and Aaron met us there. Except this time she was crying and stuff, Becca said."

"Aaron?" Tracie had never said he was at the Jacuzzi with her last week. And she hadn't mentioned drinking that night at all. Sienna had thought that they told each other everything, that there were no secrets between them. Why didn't Tracie tell her Aaron was at the Jacuzzi? "Did something bad happen between Tracie and Aaron that night?" Sienna asked George.

"I don't know. I don't think so. He drove her home from the Jacuzzi."

Sienna's mouth dropped.

"Tracie didn't tell you?" George asked.

"Nope." Apparently, she wasn't as close to her best friend as she'd believed. "Aaron's not here tonight, is he?" George asked.

"Not unless he sneaked on the boat somehow. I can't stand the guy. There's no way I'd invite him."

"Well, I just thought I should let you know about Tracie," George said.

Sienna sighed. "You did the right thing. Thanks. I'd better go check on her."

"Not the best way to spend your birthday party," Carter told her.

"I know." It was an awful way. *Tonight is supposed to be my night,* she thought.

"I'll come with you if you want," Carter offered.

"You can't. I think seeing you and me together would just make things worse." She turned to Becca. "Will you show me where you found Tracie?"

Becca nodded, and Sienna said good-bye to Carter and romance, and left the starry night sky to deal with her so-called best friend below deck.

She found Tracie in the rest room, standing in front of the sink, gripping the edge of it for support, and splashing water on her pallid face. She obviously had thrown up, and her new, beautiful dress had a long brown stain down its front. She must have spilled her drink on herself.

Sienna clenched her fist, but stood next to Tracie and said as nicely as she could, "Let me help you."

"Oh, you've helped me enough." Tracie was slurring her words. Her breath stank of liquor and vomit. "You two-faced backstabber. I told you how much I missed Carter, how I'd do anything to get him back. I believed you when you offered to ask him out for me. I hadn't realized you were really asking him out for yourself."

"I didn't exactly offer. You begged me to ask him to my party," Sienna said.

"If I'd known you two were going to dance in front of me like you were having sex right there on the boat, I never would have asked you to talk to him."

"We didn't dance like that," Sienna objected, though she knew they hadn't really danced like friends either.

"What exactly went on that night when you went to Juice Caboose?" Tracie started to fall, then steadied herself against the sink. "You've been so freakin' vague about it."

"*Me* vague? You didn't even tell me you were with Aaron that night."

Tracie's fist clenched like Sienna's. "Because I knew you'd be all superior and snotty about it if you found out. Just like you're acting now. Maybe if you hadn't left me on my own that night, I could have handled Aaron better. But you were too busy running off with my boyfriend."

"*Former* boyfriend," Sienna said.

"Thanks to you," Tracie said. "Stealing him from me under my nose, all the while pretending to be my friend."

She hadn't stolen Carter. Had she? She'd have to sort out everything that had happened, to figure out how she'd ended up with Carter tonight, whether deep down she knew they'd get together on her birthday, and whether it was such a terrible thing. How could the wonderful feeling of kissing Carter possibly be a terrible thing?

"You're not my friend," Tracie said.

"You're drunk," Sienna said.

"And you're a horrible, lying bitch!" Tracie shouted.

Sienna stomped out of the bathroom.

twenty-two

"Jay, no! Don't touch George's drum set," Mark told his little brother.

Lily laughed. "It's got to be so tempting, with George's drums stored here in the garage. In fact, Jay, I wouldn't mind going a little wild on the drums myself."

Mark put his arm around her. "You can always go wild on me."

"Yeah! Me too, Lily! I can show you my karate kicks!" Jay kicked his foot in the air, missing Mark's keyboard by about an inch.

"Watch it!" Mark yelled. "You need to get out of here."

"You never play with me!" Jay protested. "Your girlfriend is so much nicer than you are."

"She's the best, huh?" Mark said. Lily was so good with Jay and his other brother, Kyle, not to mention gorgeous, talented, and amazing in bed.

Jay tugged on Lily's arm. "Lily, will you live here?"

"That sounds like fun," Lily said. "It's so quiet in my house, usually just me and my twin brother."

"Let's trade!" Jay said.

Lily leaned into Mark and whispered, "I do love a good trade."

"Me too." Mark smiled.

"All right!" Jay clapped. "Lily, you can live in Mark's room at our house, and Mark can go live with your brother in your house."

Mark shook his head. "Me and Aaron under one roof? I don't think so."

"You just need to give him a chance, get to know him better," Lily said. "I bet he'd grow on you."

"Maybe so." That was a lie. He knew Aaron Bouchet well enough to be sure he couldn't stand the guy. Aaron was cocky, lazy, and a pig.

"Lily, will you make up another song about me?" Jay asked.

"Sure," Lily said.

Mark put his hand on Jay's back. "Maybe another time." He pushed him toward the door to the house. "You have to get out of the garage now. We have songs to write."

"Lily, please trade places with Mark," Jay said. "He doesn't play with us like you do."

"You'd better go, Jay," Lily said.

Mark pushed Jay a little farther and he was out the door. "Finally." Mark closed the door before running his fingers through Lily's lustrous red hair. "Sometimes I wish my brothers weren't so enamored with you, but at least they have good taste."

"Speaking of good taste," Lily said, right before kissing him. They made out for a long time, leaning against the door of the garage, their hands and lips tasting and caressing each other's bodies while they whispered and laughed and made each other breathless.

Man, she felt so good. And he wanted her so bad. Last night they had talked and danced and kissed at Sienna's party, then made love on the beach before going home. But that was last night. Mark wanted Lily again, today. "I wish there were a bed in here, or a couch," he murmured.

Her laugh was devilish. "Who needs a bed?"

He grinned.

Later, after they'd dressed each other and hugged and kissed some more, Mark remembered why Lily had come over—to work on songs together. Mark had been struggling with the melody of "Tomorrow." With Lily standing next to him at his keyboard and humming different tunes, he was able, finally, to get the melody just right. They worked on the lyrics together also, and Mark knew the two of them could turn "Tomorrow" into a great song.

Things seemed to be going so well between them. They were best friends, lovers, and music partners. She seemed more serious about doing her best for the band now. His parents had stopped asking about Sienna and accepted that

Lily was his girlfriend. Even Sienna appeared to be, if not warming up to her, at least not as cold as she used to be. His brothers adored her. Everyone in his family liked Lily.

"I really appreciate your help on 'Tomorrow,'" Mark told Lily as he drove her home. "You don't know how long I was struggling with that song. I thought I'd never figure out the right melody."

"But why struggle with it if we aren't going to use it?" Lily said.

"What do you mean?"

"Steve Guyda wants us to play Daybreak's bubble-gum pop crap, not our own stuff. He thinks it's, like, horrible if we try to do something creative and unique." Her voice had an edge to it.

He reached for her hand, but she moved it away. So he tried to comfort her with words. "Guyda's plan is to make us successful commercially," he said. "After that, we can experiment more."

"And your plan is to go along with his plan." Her voice wasn't merely edgy now. It was tinged with anger.

Mark tried to keep his voice calm. "Guyda's a pro, Lily."

"And you're an artist. At least I thought you used to be."

He stared at the road ahead. He wanted to grab her hand, tell her that she was right, that they had to be true to their music, that he'd stand up to Guyda so she'd be happy. But he also wanted Amber Road to be a success. He had dreamed of getting a professional manager, and now that they had one—a good one—he refused to blow that relationship. He wasn't going to disregard Steve Guyda's advice and chance losing him and thereby a shot at stardom. Mark loved Lily, but he would not risk his music career just to please her.

"You should be assertive with Guyda," she urged him. "You should insist on using all our own stuff at The Spot tonight. We've worked so hard on those songs."

Lily was asking for way too much. She didn't care about Amber Road like he did. To Lily, the band was a hobby. To him, it was the most important thing in his life. Or it used to be, anyway, before he fell in love with Lily.

He tried to reason with her. They were nearing her house, and he hated for her to leave angry. "We can sing a couple of our songs," Mark said. "Guyda still likes 'Beautiful Girl.' And maybe we can do 'School's Out' too."

"Two entire songs. Wow." Lily rolled her eyes. "Do you want to be true to your art or be a pop star?"

"Both," he said.

"That's impossible with Guyda managing us."

"Then I guess I'd like to be a pop star first, artist second." His voice remained calm, but his fingers clenched the steering wheel. "Kind of like Justin Timberlake."

"Justin Timberlake. You wish. More like one of those washed-up short-term stars no one remembers. With Guyda ordering us around, we might be famous for teenybopper songs for about five minutes. But we'll never create anything worthwhile, and we'll become has-beens while we're still teenagers."

"Lily, give me a break." He couldn't maintain the false calm in his voice anymore. He seethed as he said, "The music business involves a lot more than art. That's why they call it the music *business* rather than music *art* or something."

"Stop acting so condescending toward me." She crossed her arms. "Just because I'm not an honor student like you, doesn't mean I'm stupid."

As he pulled up to her house, he felt sick to his stomach. Man, a few hours ago they were making love, and now they acted like they hated each other. This was not how he wanted to end what had been a perfect day. "I know you're not stupid," he told Lily. "I just . . . Look, I've been in this band a lot longer than you have. I'm the one who formed it. I was smart enough to pick you for lead singer. That was the smartest thing I ever did, in fact, besides kissing you that first night on the beach."

"I kissed you first," she said.

"Lily, please, can't you trust me on this decision to follow Guyda's advice?"

"Advice? He doesn't give you advice. He gives you orders, and you follow them no matter what." She quickly got out of his Camry, slammed the car door, and rushed up her driveway.

Mark turned off the ignition and left the car without even bothering to close the door. He followed her to her house as fast as he could. "Lily," he said to her back. "I can't stand that you're mad at me. Please, let's talk."

But she didn't turn around or even glance his way. Instead, she stormed into her house and slammed the front door also.

He hurried to the door and opened it. Aaron stood in front of him, blocking his way. Mark tried to peer around Aaron, but he wouldn't move aside. "Lily!" Mark called. "Come on, Lily, we need to talk!"

"Get lost," Aaron said. "Can't you see my sister doesn't want to speak to you?"

"Aaron, please."

"Get out," he said.

Mark stayed where he was. He tried to reason with Aaron. "I don't want to leave with your sister angry at me. Please let me come in, just for a few minutes."

Aaron shook his head. "You wouldn't even let me into your stupid garage. And now you want me to let you into my house? No freakin' way, loser."

Mark tried to act calm, even though he felt like shoving Aaron hard. "Come on," Mark said. "Let me in."

"No." A slow, wide smirk spread across Aaron's face.

The guy was such an ass. But Mark held in his temper as best he could. "Aaron, please. I need to talk to her. I love her."

Aaron rolled his eyes. "You don't know the meaning of the word. You love to get into my sister's pants. That's what you love. You don't love her anywhere near as much as I do. Lily and I used to spend a lot of time together. Now she's too busy with you and your loser band."

"It's not a loser band," Mark said through clenched teeth. "And how Lily chooses to spend her time is her choice, not yours."

"Whatever. You're not coming in here." Aaron pushed forward and got in Mark's face. "Especially since you wouldn't let me in your dumb-ass garage."

Mark didn't back away. He wasn't going to let Aaron or anyone else keep him from Lily. He took a deep breath to try to maintain self-control. "You know why I wouldn't let you into band practice, Aaron. You totally messed up Tracie. She doesn't want anything to do with you anymore."

Aaron snorted. "She had plenty to do with me on the way home from the Jacuzzi last week. Give her a little beer, a Porsche, and a make-out spot, and she's all mine. Hell, with Tracie, I wouldn't even need the Porsche or a make-out spot. Just the beer. Your friend is so easy."

Mark felt nauseated. He heard Lily calling his name from somewhere back in the house, but even her voice couldn't distract him from the horrible things Aaron was saying.

"Tracie is so hot," Aaron continued. "You should see the pictures I took of her that night after we fooled around and she passed out. Smoking!"

Mark hadn't felt so awful, so out-of-control angry, since Amber had died. His whole body heated up, his eyes narrowed, and his fist clenched. He grabbed Aaron by the collar of his ridiculously tight T-shirt. "You repulsive pig!" he shouted. Then he swung his fist at Aaron and smashed his face. Mark didn't let go of Aaron's shirt until blood gushed onto his hand.

Aaron was screaming and grabbing his nose, which Mark could barely see under the mass of blood. Aaron staggered back and sank to the floor.

Lily rushed up from behind him, ripped off her shirt, and pressed it to her brother's bloody face.

"I'm sorry." Mark directed his apology at Lily because he was still too angry at Aaron.

She glared at him.

"I didn't mean to . . ." Mark faltered. At the time, he did mean to punch Aaron, to try to make him suffer for what he did to Tracie. "I guess I lost control," he tried to explain to Lily. "I was just so mad."

"Get out of here, you animal!" Lily yelled.

"Please, Lily. When he told me about Tracie, especially the pictures—"

"He's bleeding all over. My brother's bleeding. I can't believe you punched him."

"I'm sorry," Mark said again.

"Get the hell out of my house!" Lily screamed while her brother held the now-red shirt against his nose.

Mark backed out of the house. Once again, Lily slammed the door.

twenty-three

After the terrible fight with Aaron and Lily, Mark waited in his Camry in front of their house. He had to talk to Lily. His heart was already bursting. If he and Lily didn't make up, his heart would break. It took all Mark's self-restraint not to force his way in to see her. His brutish behavior had already gotten him into this mess. His only hope now was to wait for Lily's anger to soften. Then he could apologize. He'd explain that he lost his temper after Aaron told him about what happened with Tracie. Then Lily would understand why he lost control.

He let ten excruciating minutes pass, then hurried out of the car again and to Lily's front door. He knocked once.

After about a minute, Lily shouted from the other side of the door, "Go away!"

No! He couldn't leave like this. "Lily, I want to apologize. To you and Aaron. I was wrong."

"Yes, you were. Okay, so you apologized. Now get out of here!" Lily yelled. Every syllable she uttered sent a stabbing pain through his heart.

"Please," he begged, knowing but not caring that he sounded pitiful. "Please talk to me, Lily. I want to explain what happened."

"I know what happened. It wasn't enough for you to go around kissing Guyda's butt the last few weeks. You had to punch my brother too."

"I'm sorry about Aaron," Mark said again, and he meant it. He wasn't sorry about Guyda though.

"Get out of here. Now," Lily said.

So he did. He turned around, shoulders hunched, and returned to his car. But he couldn't drive away. He sat in the driver's seat with his cell phone and punched in Lily's number. The phone rang and rang. He called her again, but again she didn't answer.

He didn't know what to do. All he knew was that he had to talk to her. He felt so lost. He looked out his car window, at the oak tree in front of her bedroom window.

The tree! He could climb it. He hadn't climbed a tree in ages, but he would climb the Sears Tower today if it meant he could tell Lily what Aaron had done to Tracie.

The oak tree was large, the base about half as big as his Camry, but it had low, thick branches. He started up, grabbing the lowest branch, planting his feet against the trunk, then pulling himself onto the branch. He took hold of a branch a half-yard or so higher, gripped it tightly, and climbed higher up the tree. *This is ridiculous,* he told himself, but he kept going. He slowly moved higher and higher toward Lily's window, making sure not to look down. When he got as close to her bedroom window as he could, he yelled, "Lily! Lily, open your window! I have to talk to you! I'm sorry!"

The curtain opened and she peeked out, then retreated.

"Please, Lily!" he shouted.

He waited in the tree. Finally, the curtain moved again. It was Aaron. He opened Lily's window. His face wasn't bleeding anymore, but it was puffy and dark. "Get down from my tree or I'll climb up there and throw you off!" he shouted.

"Aaron." Behind him, Lily sounded as if she was pleading.

Aaron muttered something to her that Mark couldn't make out, then closed the window and the curtain. Mark hung on to the tree for a long time, but the window curtain remained closed. He reluctantly climbed down and returned to his car.

He sat in the driver's seat for hours, hoping Lily would come out and speak to him. He thought he saw the curtain in her bedroom flutter a few times, but it never opened.

Mark decided to knock on her front door just once more.

She opened it quickly. Aaron shouted in the background, "Don't let him inside, Lily! Don't even say one word to him. I swear I'll call the cops."

"Please let me in," Mark begged.

She shook her head.

"I just want to talk to—"

"Well, you can't," she interrupted him. "Let me talk. You listen. I don't think you understand how important my brother is to me," she said. "It's obvious you put Amber Road above everything else—including me."

"That's not true," Mark said.

She held up her hand to stop him. "I'm talking, you're listening. Remember?"

He nodded.

"I put Aaron before everything else. He's my twin brother. He's been there for me all my life. No one else has. No one's even come close to what Aaron and I have. When you hit Aaron today, it was like you were attacking me," she said. "I'm through with you, Mark. And your band too."

"No, Lily," he pleaded. "Please. Let me explain. Did you hear about the pictures Aaron took? I totally lost it."

"Pictures?" She shook her head.

Behind her, Aaron grinned.

It was all Mark could do to keep himself from running in and punching Aaron again. "He said he took pictures of—"

"Get out of here, loser!" Aaron yelled before reaching in front of Lily and slamming the front door in Mark's face.

Even that didn't make Mark turn away. He stood on the front porch, hoping that somehow Lily would change her mind and let him in or at least talk to him again.

But she didn't.

Mark stumbled to his car and slowly drove away.

twenty-four

Sienna sat on her bed the day after her birthday party and called Tracie again to see how she was doing. There was still no answer, so she left another message. Maybe Tracie was in bed. It was already close to two o'clock, but she probably had a huge hangover. Tracie had been a mess last night.

The party was totally fun for her, at least. Well, not totally. There was the drama with Tracie. Why was there constantly drama with Tracie? And she had been having such a wonderful time before she found Tracie drunk in the bathroom. She and Carter had really clicked.

She kicked the side of her bed. Why did Carter have to be Tracie's ex-boyfriend? Everything was so complicated now.

The doorbell rang. Her parents were out at her sister's softball game, so she headed toward the front door. She hoped

it wasn't one of those religious fanatics trying to convert people, or those even more fanatical realtors who handed out
notepads with their names on them and talked up the virtues
of buying property in Southern California.

She peered through the peephole. She kept staring. On the
other side of her front door was Carter. He wore a red T-shirt
and faded jeans and stood with his hands behind his back.
His lips curved up in a cautious smile.

She opened the door and flung her arms around him.

"Whoa!" He had dropped his cautious smile in favor of a
giant grin. "I wasn't sure whether I should come today because
I didn't know what your reaction would be. I definitely made
the right decision."

"You had me at hello," Sienna said.

"I didn't even say hello."

They both laughed.

"Since I had you at pre-hello, I guess I didn't even need to
bring you these." Carter thrust his hands forward. In his left
hand was a teddy bear with a bright red sparkling heart that
took up most of its middle. In his right hand, he held a large
box of See's chocolates.

"Is this my birthday present?" Sienna asked.

"I gave you your birthday present last night," he said.
"CDs and a gift certificate to the guitar store."

"I know. That's why I'm confused. What are the teddy
bear and the candy for, then?"

"They're your unbirthday presents. They're just to let you
know I care about you. More than care. I'm crazy about you,
Sienna."

She took the presents, set them on the table by the door, and kissed him. It was a kiss filled with passion and longing and maybe, just maybe, love. The kiss was sweet and exciting at the same time, and very, very good.

And bad, Sienna thought. *At least in Tracie's eyes.* She might lose her best friend over this. She forced herself to pull away from Carter.

"What is it?" he asked, breathing hard.

"You know." She was breathing just as hard. "The *T* word." *Tracie.*

"Trouble." Carter sighed.

She looked him in the eyes, his bright blue, shiny eyes. "Tracie, my best friend since middle school. You dated her for most of high school. You came to Waves to see her last week."

"Sienna, I came that night to see you."

She couldn't help smiling. All along, in the back of her mind, she'd been hoping that's why he was at Waves last week.

"Tracie and I broke up and I'm over her," Carter said. "The only girl I ever think about anymore is you, Sienna. The only thing I ever think about is you. I couldn't get anything done this morning."

Sienna kept smiling. "I couldn't stop thinking about you either," she said. "I just saw you last night, and already this morning I missed you so much."

"Please just let me kiss you again," he said.

She pressed her mouth to his and they kissed again, and again, and again. She knew her romance with Carter would make Tracie angry. But she didn't care so much about that anymore. She was done feeling guilty and trying to make Tracie happy all the time. *I deserve to be happy too*, she told herself. And nothing made her happier than kissing Carter.

twenty-five

Tracie was roused from sleep by someone knocking loudly on her bedroom door. "Go away!" she called.

"Honey, it's two o'clock. Are you all right?" her mom asked.

She glanced at the clock on her nightstand. Wow. It really was two o'clock. She had never slept this late. Even so, after all that sleep, she still had a horrible hangover. Her head felt as if it were filled with those bouncing rubber SuperBalls she used to like as a kid.

"Tracie!" her mom called.

"Sorry. I was having a bad dream. I'm fine." She closed her eyes and pressed her palm over them, hoping to stop the commotion inside her head. It didn't work.

"You want me to bring in the thermometer?"

Oh, God. "No!" she shouted more adamantly than she had planned. She tried to lighten her tone. "I'll be out soon."

"All right, darling."

Darling. Ha! She pictured herself last night at the birthday party, throwing up in the trash can, cursing at Sienna, passing out as soon as she got in Carter's car for the drive home. If her mother knew what had gone on with her last night, *darling* would be about the last endearment she'd use.

Tracie forced herself out of bed. She needed to make an appearance and play nice before her mother returned with the thermometer and a ton of questions. She walked slowly to her desk, unzipped the clutch purse she'd carried last night, and pulled out her cell phone, hoping Carter had called.

He hadn't. There were three messages, all of them from Sienna, asking if she was all right.

Sienna! Her best friend. She acted so concerned now, but she hadn't been too concerned when she was dancing with Carter.

"Yoo-hoo! Tracie! Can I come in?" her mother asked from the other side of her bedroom door.

"Mom, I'll be right out!" Tracie called. She didn't want her mother to see her new dress lying on the rug and her hair a mess, or catch the stink of her morning breath muddled with rum.

She went into her bathroom and swallowed a couple of aspirin with water from the sink. Then she prettied herself up as best she could. God, her makeup was all over her face. She looked like a deranged clown. She scrubbed her face clean, leaving it sickly white. She didn't have time to apply more makeup. Then she kicked last night's dress under her bed. She heard rustling noises—from her mother, likely—just outside her bedroom. She threw on a T-shirt and cardigan and jeans.

Her mother was waiting for her in the hallway. "You look pale, Tracie," she said. Her tone was sympathetic, not suspicious.

Tracie grinned, though it hurt her face and made the SuperBalls in her head bounce even more. "I'm probably still tired from all that dancing last night."

"So you had fun at the party?" her mother asked.

"Uh-huh. The band was cool. The food was good. A lot of people were there." When was the aspirin going to kick in?

"Sienna's parents were supervising, right?"

"Of course," she said. Of course, they didn't know she'd stocked her purse with rum, and that she'd used the cola they supplied as a mixer.

Her mother smiled. "I bet Sienna just loved her special evening."

Tracie nodded. Her head felt so heavy, it hurt every time she moved it up and down. The pain wasn't just from the hangover. It was from guilt too. Sienna's evening was supposed to be special. But Tracie couldn't let her have just one perfect night. No, she had to throw up in the bathroom, call the birthday girl nasty names, and hog the spotlight once again.

"Tracie, I made lunch for you. Come have some chicken noodle soup," her mother said.

Her stomach lurched. After last night, it needed a long rest. Tracie had to get out of the house, flee her mother's radar. She should go to Sienna's anyway, and apologize. "Thanks," she told her mom. "But I promised to meet Sienna at . . ." It was probably about two-fifteen now. "At two-fifteen. I'm late." She returned to her bedroom, grabbed the dressy gold clutch she'd carried last night, which still held her wallet and keys and phone, and escaped from the house.

She could leave behind her mother and her probing questions and watchful eyes, but she couldn't abandon her conscience. God, she felt awful. As she drove to Sienna's house, she asked herself why she always had to ruin things. Last night she was supposed to reunite with Carter on the boat. Instead, she'd ended up drunk on the bathroom floor, screaming at Sienna and humiliating herself.

As she waited at a red light, she studied herself in the car mirror. She looked washed out and miserable. She remembered how excited she'd been yesterday, before she'd messed up her life once again. She had started out well, wearing that beautiful dress she and Sienna had searched the mall for, and trying to engage Carter in conversation on the way to the party. But everything she did after that was totally stupid and wrong.

Wait a minute, she thought. *What happened last night wasn't all my fault. Carter barely talked to me on the ride over. He had led me on that I was going on a date—Sienna had too—but then he acted ice cold from the first moment he picked me up. Maybe Carter and Sienna really wanted the date to be theirs all along, just like it was at the stupid French movie last Saturday.*

She remembered how jazzed Sienna acted to have Carter at her party. And once Carter got there, he couldn't take his eyes off of Sienna. He had even complimented Sienna's dress while ignoring the beautiful one that she wore. And the way Carter and Sienna danced together—like lovers, practically—was positively gross.

A car honked behind her. While she'd been trying to sort things out, the light had turned green. She gunned the engine of her Beemer and raced through the intersection. There had to be something going on between Sienna and Carter.

Tracie turned onto Sienna's street. How could Sienna double-cross her? Why did *she* have to apologize? It should be the other way around. If Sienna and Carter hadn't turned on her last night, she wouldn't have been compelled to find comfort in a drink. They were partly at fault for her misery—mostly at fault, really.

She passed McMansions squeezed together, then went up the long, narrow hill leading to Sienna's house. For all she knew, Sienna and Carter were already sleeping together. Sienna hadn't denied it last night. As Tracie drove closer to Sienna's house, her original decision to apologize turned into a plan to confront her. She would warn Sienna to lay off her boyfriend. Ex-boyfriend, but, still, Tracie had been hoping Carter would return to her. She had never suspected that what stood in her way was the person she had considered to be her best friend.

Oh, God! No! Carter's Prius was parked in Sienna's driveway. Tracie stopped her car in the middle of the street and held her head. It hurt so badly. She hurt so badly. Things were even worse than she had feared. Had Carter slept over at Sienna's house last night, or had he just come to see her again today? What mattered was that he was with Sienna now, and that was just plain wrong.

She should turn back. She couldn't face the two of them today. Maybe she could keep an ounce of dignity and pretend she'd never come here, never seen Carter's Prius in front of Sienna's house. She turned her car into the nearest driveway to make a U-turn.

Then she stopped again. Why should she slink away as if she were the guilty one here? Sienna was totally backstabbing her, and Carter was equally at fault. He was the one who drove over to Sienna's house knowing that Sienna and she were best friends.

Tracie backed up, then drove to Sienna's house and parked at the curb. She sat in the car, trying to think what she could say.

There was nothing to think about. She would just tell them how upset she was, try to make them feel as horrible as she felt. She got out of the car, rushed up Sienna's driveway, and banged on the door.

It took a while for anyone to answer. They were probably making out. "Who is it?" Sienna asked.

"Your best friend," Tracie said in an unfriendly way.

There was a minute of silence before Sienna opened the door. It was just as Tracie had thought. Her lipstick was smeared and her hair frizzy. Obviously, someone had been kissing her and putting his fingers through her hair. "I came here to apologize for last night, thinking I overreacted," Tracie said. "But I see now that I didn't. Where's Carter hiding?"

"He's not hiding," Sienna said, surprising her. She didn't sound sorry at all. "He's just not in the hallway."

"He's in your bedroom, right?" Tracie said.

Sienna didn't answer that. "Did you want to talk to him too?" Her voice was so calm.

Tracie felt herself sneering. She didn't care. They deserved to be sneered at. "Yeah, I want to talk to you both." She shouted, "Carter, come out of hiding!" The loudness of her own voice made her head hurt even more.

He emerged from the direction of Sienna's bedroom. Tracie's stomach felt worse than before. She hadn't slept with Carter in their three years together. She certainly had never thought her best friend would. "You owe me a huge apology. Both of you," Tracie said. "Going behind my back like that."

"I'm sorry," Sienna said. "We didn't plan for this to happen."

"But you could have prevented it," Tracie said.

"We didn't want to prevent it." Carter moved closer to Sienna, so that they were almost touching.

"Sienna?" Tracie asked, shocked that her friend could be so cruel.

"You broke up with him, Tracie." Sienna's voice was almost pleading. "It's not like I stole him from you."

Tracie shook her head. "That's exactly what you did."

Sienna wore an expression of pity on her face. How humiliating! "Tracie, I tried to reunite you guys," Sienna said. "I really did. And I'm sorry. But we just—Carter and I—we realized we were kind of . . ."

"Kind of what?" Tracie asked. "Kind of mean?"

"Kind of meant for each other," Sienna said.

Tracie burst into tears.

"I'm so sorry," Sienna said.

"So you're going to keep seeing each other? Carter, don't you care that we dated for most of high school? How could you betray me like this?" Tracie asked through her tears.

"Tracie, you broke up with me. And we didn't do anything to try to betray you," Carter said. "It just happened."

"Fine," Tracie said. "I hope you know you've destroyed me. I've lost my best friend and my boyfriend all in one swoop. You don't care that you made me drink myself sick last night. You don't care about me at all. If you did, you wouldn't be together."

"We didn't make you do anything last night," Carter said.

"If you hadn't been dancing like that, I never would have gotten drunk," Tracie said. "Maybe I should go find more alcohol. It's not like I can talk to my best friend about how upset I am."

"Oh, Tracie," Sienna said.

She turned around and headed for the front door, waiting for Sienna to follow her. But Sienna didn't move.

Tracie opened the door. She turned around. "You're just going to stand there? You're not going to try to stop me?"

"Tracie, I can't rescue you anymore," Sienna said. "I'm your best friend, but I'm not responsible for your actions."

Tracie hurried out the door and into her car. She slammed the car door and peeled away from Sienna's house, sobbing as she drove.

twenty-six

Tracie pressed her foot to the gas pedal. She would take care of her aching head, her aching heart. She would make herself happy, no matter how much Sienna and Carter tried to bring her down. She kept driving, past Carter's car in the driveway of Sienna's ostentatious house, to the end of the cul-de-sac, back down Sienna's block as fast as she could, to the main street, and thankfully out of the neighborhood.

She knew exactly where she was going, having been there before with Aaron when he bought a six-pack of Heineken with a fake ID. She turned into the strip mall, found the liquor store, and parked her car in front of it. She got out and waited for someone to come by.

She approached the first person who did, a chubby man older than her parents. He'd parked next to her in a black

Mercedes with a dent in the back, and nodded as he got out of his car. "Excuse me," she said. "I lost my ID. I'm twenty-one, but I look younger and get carded all the time."

He checked her out, his gaze traveling from her head to her toes and back up again. "You're twenty-one?" he finally said.

"Uh-huh." She tried to speak confidently, as a twenty-one-year-old would.

"Sure you're twenty-one. And I'm twenty-nine." He laughed.

She didn't want to joke around. She wanted a drink, ASAP. "So I was wondering . . ."

"You want me to buy you liquor," the man said.

At least she wouldn't have to beat around the bush. "I have money. Could you buy me a bottle of wine?"

"Wine, huh? Is that what all the cool twenty-one-year-olds are drinking?" He winked at her.

If Sienna were here, they'd make gagging noises or they'd be giggling, and they'd drive away together fast. But Sienna was not here. Sienna was home, probably making out with Carter. Sienna had stabbed her in the back.

And Tracie's craving for alcohol right now was larger than her concern for her self-respect. In fact, her craving for alcohol was larger than anything. So she kept standing in front of the irritating man in the parking lot, waiting for an answer from him.

"What kind of wine you want?" he asked her. "Cab? Merlot? Pinot?"

"Huh?"

The man laughed again. "Look, I'm not buying you a thing. Do you know what happens if I buy you booze and you get drunk and do something stupid? I get sued. Ticketed too. Furnishing alcohol to a minor. What are you? Sixteen? Seventeen? Why don't you go home and read a teenybopper magazine or write in your little diary and drink some fruit punch or something? You're lucky I don't call the police."

"Thanks for nothing," Tracie said. *Jerk,* she said to herself.

She got back in her car. Maybe she should just drive home. Amber Road was supposed to perform at The Spot tonight. She shouldn't drink too much before that.

But she wanted something to help her relax before performing, especially if she had to be on the same stage as Sienna. She didn't need an entire bottle of wine. She could drink just a little, a couple of beers or maybe some rum. It would feel so good coursing down her throat and settling in her body, make her happier and calmer and better able to deal with the crap Carter and Sienna were pulling on her. She didn't want to risk drinking at home because her parents were probably there. She had to get a drink from somewhere else as soon as possible.

Tracie watched the obnoxious man drive away. She hated men. Most of them, anyway. She liked Mark and George and Brandon the bartender and her father, who would be heartbroken if he ever found out who his little girl had become. She felt she needed a drink more than ever now.

But how would she get it? She didn't look twenty-one. The only way she could think of was to just take it. She could hide a small bottle under her cardigan. She'd never shoplifted before, but stealing a bottle of wine wasn't bad compared with some other things she'd done. She'd sunk so low already.

She rushed into the liquor store before she could change her mind. A few other people wandered the aisles, fortunately, so maybe the clerk wouldn't pay attention to her. She glanced at the checkout area. A woman stood next to the cash register reading a magazine.

Tracie went to the back of the store and looked for something small and easy to drink without a mixer or a bottle opener. God, there was nothing. Everything was so bulky. And the more time she spent in here, the greater the chance the clerk would look up from her magazine and become aware of her.

She grabbed a bottle of $4.99 wine with a screw-off top. It probably tasted gross. She held it in front of her. What was she doing? She was an honor student who had never even cheated on a test, and now she was going to steal cheap wine? But she had to have a drink today or she'd go crazy.

She slipped the bottle between her T-shirt and sweater, then held it tight against her side and hurried out of the liquor store, through the parking lot, and into her car. She rushed inside and locked the doors. Her body stiffened as she stared in the rearview mirror, checking to see if anyone came out of the store to hunt her down.

She drove her Beemer to the other side of the parking lot, close to a supermarket. Then she unscrewed the cap of the cheap wine and took a big gulp. It was saccharine sweet, but that didn't stop her from drinking more of it. She drank enough to take the edge off.

She tried to decide what to do about Sienna and Carter. Should she call them right now? Yell at them? She didn't know what to do. All she knew was that she felt awful. The wine wasn't making the hurt go away. She drank some more. She wondered if Carter was still at Sienna's house. She gulped down more wine. She imagined Aaron in his bedroom, ogling the pictures of her. She chased that thought with more wine.

The bottle was half-empty before she screwed the lid back on and set it on the passenger seat. She shut her eyes and enjoyed the warm comfort the wine had provided. She knew the feeling would be fleeting, that soon she might get sick and later she'd have a hangover. So she tried to appreciate the state she was in now. She leaned back in her seat.

Someone was tapping on her car window. Oh, God, she must have fallen asleep. She sat up and looked to see who was there.

Brandon, the bartender from Waves, stood facing her. What was he doing here?

She tried to open her window, before remembering she would have to start the car for that. She fumbled to turn the key in the ignition. God, she must be wasted. Her stomach growled, reminding her she hadn't eaten all day. Finally, she started the car. She opened the passenger window by mistake. At last, she found the correct button and opened the driver's window.

"Tracie, are you all right?" Brandon looked so . . . so serious. Usually, at Waves, he wore a grin and joked around.

"What are you doing here?" Tracie asked him. She knew she sounded snarly, but she was in no mood to act nice.

"Grocery shopping." He was squinting at her as if she were a puzzle he was curious to solve. "I live a half mile away." He stared at the wine bottle in the passenger seat and tilted his head. "Then I saw your BMW."

"Well, I guess you need to get to the market now," Tracie said. She was in no mood for chitchat.

"Why are you drinking alone in your car?"

"That's none of your business," she snapped.

"I'm sorry. I'm worried about you is all," he said. "I'm a bartender, Tracie. I've seen people really go downhill with alcohol. You shouldn't be drinking."

"I get nagged enough by Sienna," she told Brandon. "And she doesn't really care about me. If she did, she wouldn't be with my ex-boyfriend right now. So don't you start nagging me too. I'll sober up. I didn't drink that much," she lied.

She glanced at the clock on her dashboard. Oh, sheesh. She must have been sleeping for a lot longer than she'd thought. "Look, Brandon, I need to go. We're booked at The Spot tonight. I only have a half hour to get ready. I'll see you at Waves next week," she told him before starting her car.

He didn't move away. "You can't drive after drinking half a bottle of wine."

"God, now you sound like Mark. Stop the nagging already," she said.

He reached his hand inside the car and tried to get her keys.

She started closing the window. "Knock it off!" she screamed.

He yanked his hand back and she closed the window all the way. "Tracie!" he yelled.

"Get out of here!" She gunned the engine, put the car in reverse, and backed out of the parking spot.

She put her car in Drive and looked ahead. Brandon stood in front of her Beemer. The jerk was trying to block her.

She slowed down, but didn't stop. She'd had enough of guys trying to tell her what to do: Mark, Aaron, Steve Guyda. The last thing she needed was Brandon not even letting her drive her own car to a very important club date.

He stood in front of the car until it was only inches away. Then he moved out of the way, finally, and she left the parking lot. She wasn't going to be late to The Spot. She'd caused enough trouble for the band. She wasn't about to blow tonight's show.

Although she didn't know how she could stand being on the same stage as Sienna tonight. Carter had better not come. What a couple of asses they'd turned out to be. She punched the steering wheel.

Oh, God! The car had careened onto the sidewalk somehow. "No!" Tracie cried out right before she crashed into a palm tree and smashed her head into the windshield.

She heard shattering glass.

Then nothing.

twenty-seven

Sienna arrived at The Spot a half hour before Amber Road was supposed to go on. The band onstage was good, so she didn't mind sitting in the greenroom and listening to the music. The band was playing a ballad called "The End." *What happened yesterday and today between Tracie and me*, she thought, *might be the end of our friendship*. After her parents had come home and Carter had left, Sienna's mood had alternated between ecstasy about Carter and sorrow about Tracie. All day her emotions had seesawed up and down.

"Sienna, what's wrong?" George asked her.

She had been focusing so hard on Carter and Tracie and the sad music playing onstage, she hadn't even noticed George enter the room.

"I'm fine," she said.

Mark arrived next, with hunched shoulders and hesitant steps, looking as sad as Sienna felt.

"Dude," George said. "What is this? National Depression Day? Or did someone forget to tell me a meteor was on its way to destroy the planet?"

"Sorry," Mark said.

"I bet I can cheer you up," George told Mark. "Our website hits are really growing and we've got a lot more friends on MySpace. People are downloading our music too, more every day. They must be recommending it like mad. Word of mouth, baby!"

"That's great," Sienna said.

Mark remained silent. "So, where's your girlfriend?" George asked him.

His response was a heavy sigh.

Had Mark and Lily broken up? Was that why Mark's eyes had been dull and his face gray since he'd stepped into the greenroom?

"I don't know if Lily will come tonight. Or any night. She's really mad at me," Mark said.

What could Mark possibly have done to upset Lily? He was such a kind person. To think about him hurting her was almost unimaginable.

"Sienna, you might have to take over as lead singer tonight. Is that okay?" Mark asked.

"I guess," she said. A month ago she would have been thrilled if Lily had broken up with Mark and left the band. Sienna had been dying to reunite with Mark and reclaim her spot as lead singer. But now she just felt sorry for Mark. And for Lily.

The door to the greenroom swung open and Steve Guyda rushed in. "Tonight's the big night! You guys are going to shine, I know it. You kids ready? I hope you've been practicing those Daybreak songs I gave you." He looked around. "Where's the rest of the band? Tell me that Tracie and Lily are in the bathroom or parking their cars, and that they'll be right here."

Mark shook his head. "I'm really sorry, Steve. Lily got upset with me today and quit the band."

"What? Upset?" Guyda asked. "Call her up and get her over here," he ordered.

"I've been trying to call her all day." Mark's voice sounded ridden with pain. "She won't pick up her phone."

"What's her number? I'll call her." Guyda whipped out his cell phone.

"No," Mark said. "To be honest, part of the reason she's upset is because she thinks I should stand up to you. If you call her and try to order her around, you'll just make things worse. Steve, you may be great at schmoozing club owners, but I got to tell you, you need to treat us better."

"You're lucky I haven't cut you kids from my client roster. Without me, this band would still be playing at high school dances. I don't think you appreciate that," Guyda said.

"I'd appreciate it a lot more if you weren't so bossy," Mark said. "The last thing that's going to make Lily come out here after I punched her brother is you yelling at her."

What? Sienna's mouth dropped open. *Mark punched out Aaron? Holy crap. No wonder Lily was mad.* Sienna wanted to applaud Mark.

"You punched Lily's brother?" Guyda asked.

"I . . ." Mark took a deep breath and stared at his feet. "I hadn't planned to. He just got me really angry about something."

"I told you the band needed to work well together, to try to get along." Guyda shook his head. "I don't know why I put up with this crap."

"You put up with it because you think Amber Road could make you some big money someday. That's why," George said.

"Sure, if you don't kill each other first," Guyda said. "Speaking of unstable band members, where's Tracie?"

The group looked at each other with puzzled expressions. "She'll be here," Sienna said more confidently than she felt.

"She'd better," Guyda said.

How could Tracie miss their big performance? Was she staying away because she was so upset about finding Carter at her house today?

Neither Lily nor Tracie showed up. Not at ten minutes before they were due onstage, when Mark phoned Lily and Sienna phoned Tracie, and both of them had to leave messages. Not at five minutes before their scheduled performance, when Guyda shouted that he couldn't believe they could be so irresponsible. Not at one minute before the gig, when Guyda said they'd have to perform as a trio.

"I'll call one more time," Sienna said. She pressed Tracie's cell phone number, hoping to apologize at least.

Tracie's mother answered. "Who's this?" she said, sounding frantic.

"Mrs. Grant, it's Sienna. I need to speak to Tracie," she said.

"Tracie's in the hospital."

"What?" Sienna felt her knees wobble.

"She crashed her car into a tree. She's at Sharp Hospital. I just got here. I have to go." She hung up.

Sienna froze, still holding the phone to her ear.

"We have no time to wait for the girls. You kids are up," Guyda said. "Just get onstage and play with three band members. Why do you have to make everything so hard for me?"

"I can't perform," Sienna said. "Tracie crashed her car. She's in the hospital."

"Un-freakin'-believable," Guyda said.

"Is Tracie okay?" Mark asked, his face even grayer than before.

"I don't know." Sienna shook her head. "I have to go see her."

"*After* your performance," Guyda said. "The show must go on."

"No. Now," Sienna said.

As she left the room, Mark and George went off with Guyda to find the club manager. She heard Guyda tell them, "You have a hell of a lot of explaining to do."

twenty-eight

Tracie lay in the hospital bed, her leg in a cast. They had patched her up and said she probably could go home tomorrow. Go home to what, though? Mark was always warning her and the rest of the band members against drunk driving. She used to think he was being paranoid. Now she found him prescient. But it was too late. He would be so mad when he found out.

Tracie wondered if Mark and the others would kick her out of the group. How could she perform onstage, anyway, with a broken leg and a banged-up face? As if drunk driving weren't bad enough, she hadn't worn a seat belt and her head had crashed into the windshield. They hadn't let her look at herself in the hospital, but she suspected she looked ghastly. Her mother had gasped when she saw her. At least she wouldn't have to hear Aaron calling her Gorgeous Girl anymore. Now she was probably Gory Girl.

Ugh. Aaron. She didn't want to think about that bastard, or Carter, or Sienna. And she was too mortified to ever go to Waves again and chance running into Brandon. He had tried to stop her from driving drunk, but she had stubbornly and stupidly pulled away from him. She groaned.

"Are you all right?" her mom asked from the chair next to her bed.

"Oh, Mom, I'm so sorry. You must be really angry."

"I'm shocked, Tracie. Truly shocked," her mother said. "We'll discuss the drinking later, when you're out of the hospital. Believe me, your father and I will have a long talk with you." She shook her head. "Thank God you're going to be okay, and no one else was hurt."

Someone knocked on the door to the hospital room. "Come in," her mother called.

Brandon stepped into the room.

"Who's this?" her mother asked Tracie.

"Brandon Cunningham." He leaned down, reached across the bed, and stuck his hand out to shake Tracie's mother's hand. "I'm a friend of Tracie's."

Her mother didn't take his hand. "You look rather old to be in high school," she said coldly.

"I know Tracie from Waves. I tend bar there."

Her mother stood up and crossed her arms. "Are you the one who's been plying my daughter with alcohol? You know it's illegal to serve drinks to a minor?"

Tracie had obviously lost all her mother's trust. And so had anyone associated with her. She said, "Brandon tried to stop me from drinking and driving, Mom. He's never given me a drink."

"Then where did you get it?" her mother asked.

Oh, God. If her mother knew she had stolen it from the liquor store, she would be ashamed of her all over again. Tracie felt a tear rolling down her face. She swiped at it. When her finger made contact with her cheek, she winced in pain.

Brandon sat down in the plastic chair opposite Tracie's mother. What a contrast between Brandon's large, muscular frame, and the small, flimsy chair. Even in her sad state, Tracie found the sight of him in the hospital chair comical. "I bet Tracie's learned her lesson," Brandon said.

"I certainly hope so." Her mother's arms were still crossed.

I made such a huge mess of everything, Tracie chided herself. She hated that her mother now knew what a loser she was. Her parents used to be so proud of her.

"Well, I just came by to see how you were doing. I keep seeing you hit that tree." He winced. "They wouldn't let me ride in the ambulance."

"It was nice of you to come," Tracie said. "I'm supposed to get out of here tomorrow. I have a broken leg and a bunch of bruises, plus a concussion, but supposedly I'll be all right." At least physically. She didn't know if she'd ever fully heal emotionally.

"What a relief there's no permanent damage," Brandon said. "And don't worry, Tracie, I didn't tell anyone at Waves."

"You've been so nice to me." She wiped a tear from her cheek. "The person you've known this past month isn't the real me," she told Brandon. "At least I hope it's not."

"Tracie, your father and I know you're a good girl," her mother said.

"I used to be. I used to be a better person." Tracie closed her eyes, ashamed to look at anyone. "God, I hate myself now."

"I never thought you were bad," Brandon told her. "And I still like you, Tracie." He took her hand and squeezed it gently.

She squeezed it back tightly. She was so grateful for him.

"We're going to get you back to your old self," her mother said. "Where is Carter, anyway? I haven't seen him much lately, except the night you two went to Sienna's birthday party. Did you two have a fight? Is that what this is all about?"

Her mother was so out of it. But Tracie pondered her mom's question just the same. *Was* this all about her and Carter? Could she ever get back to her old self?

Honestly, Tracie didn't think so. Her old self had changed a long time ago, while she was still dating Carter. During the last few months of their relationship, Tracie had been getting tired of her old self, and of Carter, and of the two of them together. She'd felt trapped by her former lifestyle. Was reuniting with Carter really going to make her happy?

There was another knock at the door. A moment later, before Tracie could even ask who was there, Sienna pushed open the door. She rushed to Tracie's bed and gave her a hug. "You okay, girl? What happened?" she asked. "I called and called."

"I'll leave you girls alone." Brandon stood up. "I'm glad you're going to be all right. Call me if you need anything. Here's my cell number." He put a little slip of paper on the nightstand.

"Thanks for visiting." Tracie tried to smile at him as he walked out, but it hurt her cheeks.

Her mother followed Brandon out of the hospital room. Tracie wondered if she was going to give Brandon the third degree, or tell him to keep an eye on her, or both.

Sienna sat in the chair Tracie's mother had just left. "I was so worried," she said. "Thank God you're okay."

"Yeah." Tracie sighed. "I can be so stupid sometimes."

"We all do stupid things," Sienna said. "What was the bartender from Waves doing here? How did he even know you were in the hospital?"

"Brandon?" Tracie sighed again. "He saw me in the car with half a bottle of wine, and tried to stop me from driving. Brandon's been really good to me."

"Tracie, are you going to be okay?"

"I'm tired, that's all." She couldn't pour her heart out to Sienna. The thought of her and Carter together was still too upsetting.

"I'll let you rest." Sienna stood up.

Tracie felt bad. She'd been rude, after her friend had given up her Saturday night to come here. Oh, God. She just remembered this wasn't just any Saturday night. Tonight was supposed to be their big debut at The Spot. "How did the band do at The Spot?" she asked.

"Fine," Sienna muttered before heading for the door. Obviously, the band hadn't done fine.

"You did okay without me?" Tracie asked.

Sienna stared at the door and nodded.

"Stop lying to me, Sienna!" She meant about The Spot, but also about Carter.

Sienna turned around and looked her in the eyes. "I didn't want to upset you in the hospital. But we canceled the gig."

"Oh, God. I screwed everything up for the band again. I'm so sorry," Tracie said.

Sienna shook her head. "Don't apologize. Just get better."

How could she be mad at Sienna when Sienna was so nice? Maybe she hadn't stolen Carter from her after all. Was Carter even hers to steal? Would he have ever been hers again? Would she even want him back now? When he had come to Waves a few weeks ago, maybe it wasn't to see her. Her head pounded. She closed her eyes.

"Get well soon," Sienna whispered before tiptoeing out the door.

A whispered voice awoke her. "I hope I didn't wake her, Mrs. Grant." It was Lily's voice. Tracie blinked open her eyes. Lily was peeking in the doorway.

"I'm up," Tracie murmured, so Lily entered the room.

"I'm glad you're here," her mother told Lily. "Tracie tells me you two have become good friends."

"Uh-huh." Lily sounded hesitant. The fact was, they weren't good friends. Far from it. Tracie hoped Lily wouldn't tell her mother the truth, that Aaron was the one she had had all the "sleepovers" with, not Lily. But Lily just said, "I was worried about you." She stood at the foot of the hospital bed, her index finger twirling a strand of her long red hair.

"I'm so sorry about The Spot tonight," Tracie told her.

"Me too," Lily said.

Tracie's mother stood up. "I'm going to get some dinner if that's all right. I'll try to rush back."

"It's okay, Mom," Tracie said.

"I'm sure you're, like, stressed out," Lily said.

Her mother smiled wanly. "You're a sweet girl."

Sweet? Lily was pretty and talented and fun, but no one who knew her well would call her sweet. "So where's Mark?" Tracie asked, knowing that Lily wouldn't visit her at the hospital without first being prodded by Mark.

Lily shrugged.

"Didn't you two come together?" Tracie asked her.

"No. George texted me and said, like, you got hurt, so I hurried over here."

Lily had learned about Tracie's accident from George? Why hadn't *Mark* told her about it? He and Lily were inseparable. Now Tracie was really confused. "Weren't you at The Spot with the rest of the band tonight?"

Lily was silent. She twirled her hair again. Tracie had never seen her like this. She'd always seemed so confident before, as if she had everything together. Lily finally said, "I quit the band. And I'm not seeing Mark anymore."

"What?" Tracie wondered if this bizarre conversation was real. Maybe it was just a hallucination stemming from the meds the nurse had given her.

"I guess Sienna will be happy now," Lily said. "I know she hates me. And you never cared much for me either."

"That's not true," Tracie said, though it wasn't a complete lie either.

Lily shook her head. "Look at me. I'm standing over your hospital bed while your face is all bruised up and your leg is broken, and I'm whining to you about *my* problems. No wonder you and Sienna don't like me."

Tracie didn't have the energy to respond to this. She hadn't realized before that Lily had picked up on their bad feelings toward her. Now Tracie felt worse than ever.

Lily sighed. "I'll shut up now. I really did come to see how you were, because I was worried about you, not because I wanted someone to unload on."

Tracie actually liked that Lily was unloading on her. "I'm just glad someone else can be the drama queen for a change," she told Lily. "Usually that's been my job, unfortunately. Like I had to make a big, inappropriate scene at Sienna's birthday party. Talk about taking the spotlight at the totally wrong time!"

Lily sat in the chair next to the hospital bed. "Thanks for being so understanding," she told Tracie. "I'm, like, not myself today, anyway. I can't believe Mark and I broke up."

"Being without a boyfriend sucks," Tracie said.

"It isn't that. I've spent lots of time without a boyfriend before."

Tracie had spent only a little bit of time without a boyfriend, and she had been miserable for virtually every moment of it.

"I can be happy without a guy around," Lily continued. "I like being by myself or hanging with friends. My problem is . . . It's that . . ." She started crying. "It's that I don't have Mark!" Her quiet tears grew to loud sobs. "Oh my God, I'm being awful, crying about my own problems when you've been in a horrible accident."

As Tracie handed Lily a tissue from the nightstand, she tried to reconcile the confident, fun-loving Lily she thought she knew with the girl sobbing next to her. It was hard to believe Tracie would have to soothe Lily for a change. But she attempted to, anyway. "Mark's a great guy," Tracie told her. "And you two seem so in love. I hate to see you guys broken up."

"I thought we had something special." Lily sobbed.

"You do. You really do. I've been thinking about that a lot lately. I'm starting to realize that I didn't have that with Carter, at least not in the last few months we were dating. We were drifting apart. And I never had anything special with your brother, either. I liked Carter, and I lusted after Aaron. But I don't think I had real love with either one of them."

"Tracie!" Lily laughed through her tears. "Telling me about your lust for my brother? TMI! Too much information. Way too much."

Tracie laughed too. It felt as if Lily and she were close friends all of a sudden. "Sorry. But the point is, I didn't really have true love with Carter or Aaron. Not like the relationship you and Mark have. You two are totally right for each other."

"I used to think so too," Lily said. "Then he punched my brother in the face."

"*What?* Why? That doesn't sound like Mark at all," she told Lily. "He's never hit anyone, ever."

"I saw them when it happened," Lily said. "Mark and Aaron were arguing about something. I caught, like, the tail end of it. But it wasn't a physical fight until Mark suddenly swung his fist into Aaron's face."

Tracie felt worse than ever. "Aaron had to have done something awful. Mark wouldn't just punch someone out of the blue."

Lily shook her head. "Tracie, you know Aaron. He's not a straightlaced guy like Carter. But he's still basically sweet."

There was that word again, *sweet*. Lily didn't seem especially sweet, but Aaron was totally the opposite of sweet.

"I saw it with my own eyes," Lily continued. "Mark took a swing at my brother for no reason and gave him a bloody nose."

"I know you love Aaron a lot, Lily. But I've got to tell you—he isn't sweet."

"Just because he saw other girls when you were going out doesn't make him a monster." Lily took Tracie's hand and squeezed it.

Tracie took a deep breath. She owed it to Mark to show Lily how awful her brother really was. "There's more," Tracie said. "That night at the Jacuzzi? Remember I got all wasted, and Aaron offered to take me home, and he swore he'd be a gentleman?"

Lily nodded silently.

"He drove to a deserted spot and he stopped the car." Tracie's eyes filled with tears, but she pushed herself to continue talking. "Then . . ."

"Did you have sex?"

"No. I was so drunk. I let it go too far, but at least we didn't have sex."

"I'm sorry he took advantage of you," Lily said.

"It gets worse, Lily." Tears streamed down Tracie's face, but she made herself keep going. "I passed out. The next day at school, Aaron said he'd taken pictures of me. He even hinted that he could post the pictures on the Internet."

"Oh my God!" Lily cried.

"I was so embarrassed," Tracie cried. "I didn't even tell Sienna what had happened. But Mark saw me near tears at school. I bet he found out what happened, got really mad, and that's probably why he punched your brother."

"Oh, Tracie, I feel so awful." Lily's lip quivered as she spoke. "I . . . I can't upset you any more than I already have." Her voice trembled. "I was supposed to visit you to cheer you up, and now we've gotten into all this drama." She stood up and walked toward the door.

"Lily!" Tracie called after her.

"I'm so sorry." Lily left the hospital room.

Tracie didn't know what exactly Lily was sorry for. Did Lily mean she was sorry about Aaron? Maybe Lily was just sorry about everything, all the relationships that had been broken because of her idea to trade guys. Tracie had hurt

Carter. Aaron had hurt Tracie. Mark had hurt Aaron. Lily had hurt Mark. It was all a crazy mess.

Still, she wished Lily hadn't left. Tracie lay on her back staring at the ceiling, feeling hopeless. She still didn't have a boyfriend, or even a potential boyfriend. She'd treated Sienna terribly. She'd have to deal with the consequences of her drunk-driving accident—her broken leg, her wrecked car, a trip to court, and probably a large fine. She wouldn't be allowed to drive for a long time. And there was a lot more to deal with than the consequences of the accident. Tracie realized she had a drinking problem, a serious one that she'd have to fight off if she wanted to save her wreckage of a life.

Someone started to open the door to her room again. Tracie hoped Lily had returned, thanking her for telling her the truth about Aaron, promising to forgive Mark for hitting him.

Or maybe Mark was here. George had left a message for her, telling her she'd better get well soon or he'd serenade her at the hospital with Neil Diamond songs. But Tracie hadn't heard anything from Mark. Was he mad at her for ruining their chance at The Spot? She hoped he'd forgive her.

No, it wasn't Lily or Mark—only the nurse. "You just got flowers," she told Tracie. She held out a bouquet of peach roses.

Tracie sat up in bed. "They're so beautiful! Who brought them?"

"The lady from the florist shop across the street."

"Could you read me the card?" Tracie asked, pointing to the little tag taped onto the cellophane around the roses.

The nurse squinted at it. "I don't see a name. The card reads, 'Tracie. Get better soon. You're a wonderful person who deserves the best.' "

Who had sent the roses? "Are you sure there's no name?" Tracie asked.

The nurse peered at the card again. "Yes, I'm sure. No name."

Tracie thanked her and stared at the ceiling again. She still felt bad, physically and emotionally. But she no longer felt hopeless.

twenty-nine

On Sunday night, Mark sat alone on a blanket at the beach, shivering in the chilly wind, his head dropped into his hands. He looked up at the starless sky. "Help me, Amber."

He waited, silent and still, for a star to appear in the dark haze, or a bird to caw or squawk or sing, or any such sign that Amber was watching and listening to him. But there was nothing except the same cruel wind and pounding ocean waves that had menaced him for hours tonight.

Mark spoke to the black, mysterious sky. "I haven't felt so unhappy since you died, Amber. I love you so much and I miss you like crazy. And now I miss Lily too. I've lost you both."

He cried for the first time in months. On the damp, desolate sand, he didn't hold back. His shoulders shook and his tears fell onto his crossed legs beneath him. His sobs were wrenching, just as they were during the first months after Amber died.

After a long while, Mark's tears were spent and he was exhausted. He dried his face with the sleeve of his jacket, then looked skyward again. "Amber, you're gone and I can't have you back no matter how much I miss you." He slugged his fist into his thigh. "But I still have a chance with Lily. I just don't know how to get her to return to me. I wish you were still here, Amber. You would have helped me. You always were there when I needed you. I still feel your presence when I play my music. Every single time, Amber. I play for you. But it's not the same without Lily. The band needs her back. I need her back. I love her."

Mark thought he heard someone coming. He told himself to stop talking. Anyone listening to him rant would think he was crazy. Maybe he *was* crazy. It was crazy to be at the beach on this cold, windy night.

The footsteps came closer. He turned in their direction.

Oh, man. "Lily!" he shouted and sprang to his feet. He took a step toward her before stopping. Was she here to make up with him? Yesterday she was so mad. Was she ready to forgive him?

She ran to him. "I'm so glad I found you," she said.

He hugged her tight. "I missed you so much, Lily." He put his fingers through her glorious hair, touched her small shoulder, stroked her soft cheek, as if making sure it was really her, that Lily really was right here in his arms. "How did you know where to find me?"

"I just felt it," Lily said. "And we've been here before. We were here Friday night."

As if he needed to be reminded of that. "Thank you for finding me. I'm so sorry about what I did to your brother."

"It's okay," she said. They held each other for a long time.

"We should talk," Lily finally said. Mark kept an arm around her, and they sat down on his blanket as close together as they could. "I went to see Tracie in the hospital," Lily said.

Mark sighed with shame. He hadn't been able to bring himself to visit Tracie. He feared that he'd have no sympathy for her, that instead of giving her comfort he'd yell at her for drinking and driving. "Is she all right?" he asked Lily.

"She had a concussion, her face is all bruised and swollen, and her leg is broken. She's not just hurt physically. She's really been through the wringer lately." Lily took a breath. "Tracie told me about the pictures Aaron took of her when she was passed out in his car."

"I'm sorry," Mark said. He knew it must be devastating for Lily to learn that the brother she loved so much had treated Tracie so terribly.

"So now I understand why you hit Aaron," Lily said.

"I shouldn't have." Mark frowned. "I lost my temper."

"I'm just not sure I can ever forgive my brother for this." Lily started to cry. "I made him delete the pictures from his camera and his computer. I watched him do it to be sure. Oh, Mark! They were awful, awful pictures! I feel disgusted just being related to him."

"Don't." Mark stroked her hair. "I feel disgusted with myself too. I should have visited Tracie in the hospital."

Lily kissed him. On his cheek, on his lips.

The despair and anger Mark felt before he saw Lily at the beach melted away. They held each other, and he forgot all about Tracie and Aaron and, for a brief time, even Amber. The only thing that mattered to him in those incredible minutes was Lily. Luscious, lovely Lily.

thirty

When the doorbell rang Monday afternoon, Tracie was sitting at the desk in her bedroom trying to do calculus. She had let her schoolwork go for too long. It was time to get back on track. Unfortunately, her mind felt a little fuzzy from the pain pills, and it was hard to sit comfortably with her leg in a cast.

A minute or so later, her mother came into her room and asked her if she was feeling up to seeing Mark.

She bit her lip. Mark must be so angry at her. She'd ruined Amber Road's opportunity at The Spot. And she'd been driving drunk, despite Mark's many warnings not to. She thought about telling her mother that she wasn't feeling well enough for company. But Mark had made the effort to visit her. Turning him away would probably only make things worse between them. "Ask him to come in, please," she told her mother.

Tracie used her crutches to stand up. She studied herself in the bedroom mirror. She looked bad enough without makeup, but today the bruises and the swelling on her face made her appear atrocious. Well, she had a lot more to worry about than her looks. Besides, Mark was like a brother to her. Their relationship had always gone beyond appearances. Although she doubted he felt very brotherly to her now.

"How are you doing?" Mark stood at the doorway to her bedroom. He didn't seem disgusted with her, but maybe he was just hiding it well. "Lily said you got pretty banged up."

"It was sweet of her to visit me," Tracie said. "I'm doing as well as can be expected from someone with a black-and-blue face and a broken leg. But everything should heal eventually. Mark, I'm really sorry about Saturday night."

"I'm just glad you're okay," he said.

"But I ruined Amber Road's big night at The Spot. And you'd warned us so many times about drinking and driving. I totally ignored you. I'm so sorry for hurting you. I can't imagine anything worse."

"Oh, there's worse," Mark said. "We got off easy."

She made her way to her bed and slowly sat down, then gestured to her broken leg. "If this is getting off easy, I'd hate to see hard."

Mark sat down next to her on the edge of her bed. "I've seen hard. I've seen a lot harder."

"You have?" Tracie cocked her head.

"Amber—the girl I named the band after—she was in a car accident," Mark said. "A single-car accident, like yours. Except she died." He put his face in his hands. Tracie stroked his back. "Her alcohol level was over twice the legal limit." His voice was barely audible. "We were young too. Not old enough to drink legally, barely old enough to drive." Tears fell silently down his face.

Tracie put her hands over his. She wished she could capture the tears, but they kept coming down. "If only I had stopped her!" Mark cried. "I knew what Amber was doing. I caught her once late at night, about a month before she died, stumbling out of the car with breath that reeked of beer. I should have told someone. I should have taken away the car keys. I should have—"

"Don't blame yourself." Tracie put her tear-stained hand under Mark's chin and lifted his head. "It was an accident."

Mark's tears began to dwindle. "Amber wouldn't want me to live like this," he said. "Ever since she died, I've been wracked with guilt, with sadness and anger. I hoped playing my music would make me feel better. It's always something I've loved to do."

"Who was Amber?" Tracie asked.

Mark shook his head. "Amber was my best friend. We grew up together and she got me into playing keyboard. We used to jam together all the time. . . . I created the band for her. It was my way of trying to keep her alive, I guess. But I screwed that up too. I sold out. Steve Guyda wants us to sound commercial, to dumb down our sound, and I agreed. But that's not us. That doesn't honor Amber's memory at all."

"It's not too late to change things," Tracie said, thinking about her life as much as Mark's.

Mark lifted his head. "You're right." He clenched his fists. "If we don't go with our own sound, there's no point in even playing. I got so carried away with the idea of being a famous rock star that I forgot why I started the band in the first place. I just need to be more confident, in my songwriting ability and in Amber Road's unique sound."

Tracie nodded. She realized she had gone off the wrong track for similar reasons. She hadn't had confidence in herself either. She believed she needed a boyfriend to be happy, when really she needed to be happy with herself. In fact, she wasn't happy with Carter when he was her boyfriend. Near the end of their relationship, she was frustrated with his unwillingness to take risks and experiment. Carter wasn't in the wrong. It was just his way, and they had grown apart.

She remembered that night when they stood outside the Jacuzzi. She wanted to go in, but Carter and Sienna refused. It wasn't their fault. They were good people, just more cautious than she was. So why was she making such a big deal about them dating? She was so fearful of being on her own. But, really, wasn't it time to take care of herself? *It's not too late to change things,* she reminded herself, just as she'd reminded Mark.

"Tracie, you okay?" Mark asked.

She nodded. "Just kind of tired." She wasn't tired. All of a sudden, her mind was racing with ideas. She appreciated Mark coming over, but now she wanted to be alone. She had things to do to get her life back on track.

"I'll let you rest now. I need to go anyway and figure out how to revive Amber Road."

"I'll understand if you want a new guitarist," she told Mark. "I really ruined things for you guys, and I'm such a mess now."

"Are you kidding, Tracie? You have to stay in the band. Hurry up and get well so you can play again."

She reached out and hugged him.

After Mark left, Tracie reached under her bed and pulled out the last two bottles of beer she'd stashed there. She stared at them for a long time. She felt so jittery and confused. A little drink would calm her right down. She held the bottles against her chest, hobbled to her bathroom, opened them, and washed the beer down the sink. She had thought drinking would get her through hard times, but in the end it made everything even harder.

She made her way back to her bed and lay across it. Now there would be no alcohol to smooth things over, no relationship to throw herself into, no big dramatic scenes to shake things up. She would focus on being her own person—whoever that was. It scared her a little. She'd just have to rely on herself from now on. She smiled. She was looking forward to it. Sort of.

thirty-one

The crutches were a pain in the neck. On Wednesday night, Tracie had to have her mother carry her guitar into Mark's house while Tracie focused on not falling. The last thing she needed was to bruise up her face even worse or break her other leg.

"Hey, cool guitar!" Mark's brother Jay said as she hobbled in. "What happened?" Jay suddenly stared at her as if she'd just walked out of a horror movie. "Why is your face all gross?"

"Jay!" his mother said. "Don't be rude."

"It's okay. He's just curious." Tracie smiled thinly. "I wasn't careful when I drove my car. I look pretty bad, huh?"

Her mother raised her eyebrows. "I really hope you learned a lesson from this."

Tracie nodded. "Believe me, I did." If getting injured hadn't taught her not to drink and drive, her parents' endless lectures over the last few days had. And even if the injuries and lectures didn't get through to her, losing her driver's license, signing up for group counseling, having a court date scheduled, and owing her parents thousands of dollars for the damage to her car and legal fees had all taught Tracie a hard, unfortunate lesson.

"Tracie, you don't look *that* bad," Jay said. "Not like a monster or anything."

"Thanks." Tracie had to laugh. If she didn't have a sense of humor about this, she'd cry. And she'd already done plenty of that.

"Let's get you to rehearsal," Mark's mother said. They said good-bye to Tracie's mother and walked to the garage. Mrs. Carrelli knocked on the door and then left when she heard Jay calling her.

Mark opened the door. His hair was messed up and his face was flushed. Lily stood behind him, adjusting her tank top.

Tracie smiled. "I hope I'm not interrupting anything."

"Not at all," Mark said, blushing even more. Tracie thought she saw a semicircle of pink lipstick on the side of his neck.

"Hey, Tracie." Lily gave her a quick wave. "Your face is looking better already."

"Mark's brother said I don't look like a monster. I'm taking that as a compliment."

"Mark's little brothers don't hold back," Lily said. "When I came in today, Kyle said it looked like I'd grown too big for my shirt. He told me I should put it in the hand-me-down pile and get one that's not so tight."

Tracie giggled. "Maybe Mark's mother told him to say that."

George and Sienna came into the garage next. A few weeks ago, she and Sienna would have smiled at each other. But now everything had gotten so awkward. Sienna didn't even make eye contact with her.

"Hey, guys. Since we're all here, we should start practicing," Mark said. His cell phone rang. He glanced at it. "That's Guyda. I'd better pick up."

"Does he have to interrupt our rehearsal?" Lily asked. "You could wait a couple hours and then call Guyda back."

"He's our manager, Lily." Mark said tersely.

More trouble in paradise? Tracie wondered. In school the last few days, every time she'd seen Mark and Lily together, they'd been holding hands or whispering to each other or arm in arm. Tracie didn't like hearing them bicker.

Mark answered the phone. A few moments later, he shouted, "This Friday night? Are you serious? Oh, man!" Everyone stood where they were, quietly listening to the call. "Thanks for arranging the gig," Mark said into the phone. After a pause, he shouted again, "You're kidding!" Then he lowered his voice. "Of course, I know you don't kid. I'm sure we can do it. I'll call you back if there's a problem, but I know there won't be any. Everyone will be psyched about coming."

As soon as he hung up, Sienna asked, "Do you have some good news for us?"

"Very," Mark said. "We, five great musicians and singers in the band, who totally deserve this, may I add—"

"You may not add. Just get to the point!" Lily urged.

He grinned. "Okay. We're going to perform at Waves this Friday night! And get this: we're the headliners!"

"Oh my God!" Tracie exclaimed.

"Dude!" George pumped his fist.

"I guess that phone call was important after all." Lily kissed Mark on the cheek. "I shouldn't complain about Steve Guyda."

"The dude swims with the sharks," George said.

"He probably eats the other sharks whole and then spits them out in little pieces just for spite," Sienna said.

Lily laughed. "Guyda might be a jerk sometimes, but he sure knows how to get us great gigs."

"Actually, I think this one kind of fell into Guyda's lap," Mark said. "He told me that the lead singer of the band scheduled for Friday got arrested for drug dealing, so they needed someone at the last minute."

"Well, I'm glad Guyda suggested us to the club owner," Sienna said.

Mark shook his head. "It wasn't Guyda. Someone who works at Waves suggested us. Apparently, he really talked us up."

Tracie felt faint. "*Which* someone who works at Waves?"

"That bartender," Mark said. "I forget his name."

"Brandon?" Tracie asked.

Mark shrugged. "Yeah, that's it."

Tracie hadn't felt this happy in a long time. She visualized herself onstage, headlining at Waves with her guitar and her friends. But she couldn't stop imagining who would be offstage, behind the bar. She twirled her hair as she thought about Brandon, his kindness toward her, his generosity to Amber Road, and his sexy green eyes.

"Anyway, we got the gig!" Mark exclaimed. "Now we have a lot of work to do if we want to learn the songs Guyda gave us."

Lily groaned.

"I said *if* we want to learn the songs," Mark said.

Sienna cocked her head. "I thought we had to, that Guyda's insisting."

"Guyda works for us. We don't work for him," Mark said. "Right, Lily?"

She hugged him. "You got it."

"But he'll demand to see a set list before our next show," Tracie said. "If he finds a bunch of our own songs on it, he'll go ballistic."

"That's why we'll give him a fake set list," Lily said.

"What?" Mark said.

"Brilliant," George said. "Absolutely brilliant. We put all of Daybreak's dumb songs on the fake list, and then we sing our own great stuff onstage."

"So he goes even more ballistic afterward," Mark pointed out.

Sienna frowned. "I wouldn't put it past the man to rush onstage partway through our set and start yelling at us."

"He won't do that," Lily said.

"Why not?" Tracie asked her.

Lily grinned. "Because we'll do a fantastic show and have such an overwhelming response from the audience that he'll realize he was wrong to stifle our creativity."

"But what if he doesn't? What if the audience response is overwhelmingly negative? Guyda will drop us like a bad habit." Tracie had been through enough trauma lately. The last thing she wanted was for Amber Road to flout Guyda's advice, bomb onstage, and lose their manager or their support at Waves or both.

Mark put his arm around her. "You know what, Tracie? I think I'd rather be in a struggling band that does its own thing and risks losing its manager than in a successful bubble-gum pop band."

"Well, I wouldn't mind having a few bestselling bubble-gum pop songs and making ten mil or so while I'm still a teenager," George said. "In fact, if Steve Guyda can make us rich and famous, I'd be okay if he told us to go onstage naked and rock out to Engelbert Humperdinck songs. Then I could retire to a mansion on the beach in Maui and create unique music that doesn't sell."

Everyone laughed.

George put up his hand and continued talking. "But I think we can try to have our own sound *and* be successful. Let's go for it."

"I'm up for that," Sienna said.

"Me too." Tracie smiled, pain free. The bruises on her face were healing quickly.

"Okay, guys," Mark said. "Which songs of ours should we practice? 'Rock It Like a Rocket?' 'Stray Cat?' 'Beautiful Girl?'"

"All of them," Tracie said. There was nothing she wanted more right now than to make great music with her friends.

thirty-two

Sienna was so excited! In a few hours, Amber Road would be playing at Waves as Friday night's headliner.

Things weren't perfect, of course. Tracie was in a cast and would have to sit in a chair onstage. At least she could still play guitar, and her bruises were healing. Sienna wondered how Tracie felt inside though. She had always been so emotionally fraught. Finding Carter at her house and getting in a drunk-driving accident could only have made things worse. Sometimes Tracie was high-strung and needy, but Sienna still missed her best friend like crazy.

Sienna walked with her cell phone to the backyard for some peace and privacy, and gave Tracie a call.

"Sienna?" Tracie sounded cautious when she picked up, but at least she didn't seem angry.

"How are you feeling?"

"A lot better," Tracie said. Sienna wasn't sure if that meant physically or emotionally, and didn't want to ask.

"I was thinking that before we go to Waves tonight, I could do your makeup," Sienna suggested. Given that Tracie's face was still a bit black-and-blue, Sienna suspected she could use the help.

Tracie didn't respond.

Sienna wasn't giving up. "You know, I learned a lot from being on stage crew for *A Midsummer Night's Dream* last year. Remember, you said I even managed to make the Rainer twins look attractive."

Tracie laughed. "I guess if you could pull that off, you could make me look good."

"You already look good. Great, really. I just thought I could make you look even better."

"Thanks for offering, but I don't want your help anymore," Tracie said. "I'm trying to be more independent."

Sienna's mouth dropped. She hadn't been sure whether Tracie would accept her offer or tell her to go to hell. But she never expected her to say she wanted to be more independent. "You're in a cast," Sienna told her friend. "And you can't even drive. You've got to accept some help."

"I don't need the use of my leg to put on makeup," Tracie said.

"Fine. Be that way," Sienna said.

Tracie sighed. "I didn't mean to be obnoxious. I really appreciate your offer. How about you just come over and hang out? Actually, I want to talk to you about something."

"I'll be there in about twenty minutes," Sienna said before hanging up.

As she knocked on the front door, Sienna wondered if this would be the last day she'd ever be at Tracie's house. In a few minutes, Tracie might tell her that she never wanted to be friends with her again.

When Tracie let her in, she was smiling; it was a thin smile but a good sign nonetheless.

"I take it your parents are at the movies," Sienna said.

"It's Friday night." Tracie walked on crutches toward the kitchen. "You know my parents. They're at the movie theater every Friday like clockwork."

Sienna followed her into the kitchen and sat at the table. How could she lose someone who was so close to her that she even knew her parents' schedule?

"Want a drink? Cookies?" Tracie took a metal tin from the kitchen counter, set it in front of Sienna, and lifted the lid.

Sienna peered into the tin before grabbing a large chocolate chip cookie. "Did your mom make these?"

"I did," Tracie said.

"No way." Sienna rolled her eyes.

"Seriously, I baked them myself."

Sienna bit into the cookie in order to keep her mouth from dropping again. She made a thumbs-up sign as she ate it. "That was delish," she said, licking the crumbs from her lips. "But Tracie, you always say you don't know how to cook. Remember the only B you ever got was in Home Ec in middle school?"

"Part of my plan to be more independent." Tracie hobbled over to the refrigerator and poured Sienna some milk. "I know you love milk and cookies."

"And these cookies are really good." Sienna took another one.

"Well, enjoy. I proved to myself that I could bake something, but I also confirmed I hate to cook." She smiled. "So I'm on to new challenges."

"Such as?" Sienna asked.

Tracie sat down next to her, laying her crutches on the floor. "New challenges such as learning to like myself whether or not I have a boyfriend. Such as realizing that I had already drifted away from my ex-boyfriend months ago. Such as letting him go, finally. New challenges such as trying to be as good a friend to you as you've been to me all these years. Though I know I could never be as kind and generous as you are. Such as telling you I'm okay with you going out with Carter." Tracie shrugged. "And, I'm not sure if I'm mature enough yet for this, but I hope that seeing you two happy together will just add to my own happiness."

Sienna jumped up from the table and hugged her.

Tracie hugged her back just as hard. "I'll tell you what," she said. "You do my makeup and I'll do your hair."

So Tracie put Sienna's hair into an elaborate French braid, tucking a peach rose in her hair. Then Sienna gently put makeup on Tracie, and Tracie put a rose in her own hair. "Your father sure grows nice roses," Sienna told her friend.

"Those are from a bouquet I got in the hospital," Tracie said.

Sienna raised her eyebrows. "A bouquet from who?"

"There was no name on the card, but I have a feeling I know who the roses are from." She smiled as she talked.

"Who?" Sienna asked again.

Tracie kept smiling. "A great guy. I'll tell you who as soon as I know for sure. I know I'm supposed to be independent, but can you drive me to Waves?"

"Of course." Sienna returned Tracie's smile. "But only if I can have another one of those cookies you baked, since you're never going to cook again."

As Sienna drove Tracie to Waves, they spent most of the ride laughing.

Steve Guyda was already at the club when they arrived, standing in the front row, clutching the fake set list Mark had given him. The list was replete with songs from Daybreak, most of which the band hadn't even bothered to learn.

Sienna's worries about tricking Guyda dissolved as she gazed at the audience. What a rush! The club was packed with people who had come especially to hear them! Guyda had been right about them needing to promote themselves. They had put out the effort and it had succeeded, big time. And it wasn't just their classmates here: people from other schools had shown up too. The Amber Road website had been getting hundreds of hits a day and they had hundreds of friends on MySpace. Sienna even heard two strangers talking about Amber Road at Starbucks this morning before school. Best of all, in Sienna's opinion, was seeing Carter, a few rows back in the center, staring at her with his striking blue eyes.

The warm-up band finished onstage and received mild applause. As Amber Road gathered up their instruments, some people near the front of the room started singing "Beautiful Girl." At least half the audience joined them, many of them holding up Amber Road keychains and stickers.

"Let's go!" Mark called. They went onstage with their real set lists. Sienna knew if they screwed up tonight, Guyda would go nuts.

Sienna helped Tracie into the chair and set down her crutches next to her. "You going to be okay playing like this?" she asked.

"Yeah," Tracie said. "I'm just so happy I get to play at all. You guys always stand by me, no matter what crazy messes I get myself into."

"I'll stand by you no matter what," Sienna said. "But I hope you don't get into any more crazy messes. For your own sake, mostly. I care about you."

"Thanks for being my friend," Tracie said.

"Three, two, one!" Mark shouted.

Sienna and Tracie smiled at each other.

"Rock!" Mark screamed. And they began. They started with "Rock It Like a Rocket," one of only two of their own songs on the fake set list they'd given Guyda. The crowd went wild.

Then they played the next song on the fake set list, one written for Daybreak. It got tepid applause and a few puzzled looks from fans familiar with Amber Road's music.

After that, they played their own stuff for the rest of the night: "Kiss Me," "Stray Cat," "Don't Leave," "Partytime," and of course, "Beautiful Girl." They totally hit their stride, and the audience cheered them on with unflagging spirit.

Mark and Lily sang their duets in perfect synch, and when Sienna joined her voice to theirs, the songs never sounded better. A month ago, Sienna had considered Lily a hateful person and found being near Mark agonizing. Now she had forgiven both of them.

It was more than that. She was genuinely happy they had found love with each other.

Sienna thought that Tracie had changed too, in a good way. She had matured. She no longer seemed like a little girl lost without a boyfriend to follow. Tracie had become her own person, and proven herself as a true friend.

Behind them, George played his drums with vigor and passion. They had all come together as if they'd never had any trouble before. A month ago, they had merely been trying to hold on. Now, Sienna felt she and her friends were soaring.

Sienna loved being onstage from start to finish. But also, she couldn't wait for their set to end, so she could talk to Carter and feel his warm touch.

thirty-three

After helping Tracie offstage, Mark went straight to the greenroom. He couldn't wait to celebrate the band's success with Lily—kiss her, hug her, be with her! After nearly losing her this past week, Mark wanted to savor every minute with her now.

But she wasn't there.

Steve Guyda had made it backstage though, pacing from one side of the small room to the other with his arms crossed. He didn't even say hello. Instead, he asked, "What the hell happened to the set list, to all the Daybreak songs you promised to play?"

Mark shrugged. "We sang one of them."

"One! One!" Guyda shook his head. "Musicians! A bunch of bullheaded nutcases!"

Mark kept calm. If wanting to play his own songs made him a bullheaded nutcase, then so be it. "We did okay, though, Steve."

Guyda gave him a thin smile. "I don't like to say I'm wrong. So I'll just say you were more right. Okay. Do all your own songs from now on."

Mark returned the smile with a wide one of his own. "Thanks, Steve."

"We rocked!" Sienna said next to them. She and Mark gave each other high-fives. Maybe they could be good friends again one day. Mark certainly hoped so.

"Hey, don't forget me," George said behind them.

"And me," Tracie said. So Mark gave them high-fives too.

The bartender came into the greenroom with a tray full of glasses of soda and water.

"Brandon, you're so thoughtful," Tracie gushed. Her eyes were bright and a smile spread across her face. Mark hadn't seen her so happy in a long time. "I don't know what's nicer, delivering drinks to us backstage or sending me flowers when I was in the hospital."

Whoa! How long had this been going on? Mark barely knew the guy.

"You're a great girl, Tracie," the bartender said. "And you really blew the audience away tonight. Even with a cast on your leg. You blew me away, Tracie. You always do."

"You're sweet," Tracie told him. "If I didn't have these crutches, I'd hug you."

"I think we can manage that anyway." Brandon reached down and gave her a hug.

"Thanks a lot for the referral here, Brandon," Mark said. "I heard you really went to bat for us. And you're right: Tracie was awesome on guitar tonight."

Tracie didn't say anything. Mark didn't think she was listening to him. She was staring at Brandon with bright eyes and red cheeks. It was about time something good happened to her. Mark just hoped Brandon was a decent guy. He'd hit his quota of people to punch on Tracie's behalf.

"I'd better get back to the bar." Brandon left the room.

After the door closed, Mark told Tracie, "This guy had better treat you well."

"Hey, it's not like Brandon and I are dating or anything," Tracie said, but she was beaming.

"Speaking of dates, where's mine?" Mark asked. "I haven't seen Lily since we were onstage."

"I saw her talking to some dude near the back of the room," George said.

"I'll go find her." Mark walked toward the door.

Just then, Lily showed up. Mark hugged her and asked her where she'd been. "Oh, just talking to a fan," she said.

"Kids, you were awesome tonight," Guyda said. "You almost gave me a stroke when you ignored the set list you gave me, but it all worked out for the best. I want to set up a lot more gigs for you kids, maybe for some clubs in L.A. and up the coast."

"That's great!" Sienna exclaimed.

"Thanks a lot!" Tracie said.

Mark and George gave each other high-fives again.

While everyone was celebrating, Lily rushed out of the greenroom.

Mark followed her. She headed to the back of Waves. As Mark made his way toward her, he was slowed by all the well-wishers and back-slappers along the way, congratulating him and the band on a great performance.

As he got closer to her, he noticed Lily immersed in conversation with an older guy he'd never seen before.

Someone gripped Mark's shoulder—hard—from behind. Mark turned partway around. It was Aaron. His nose was a little puffy but much improved. "Spying on Lily again?" Aaron sneered. "Too bad Waves doesn't have a tree you can climb to get a better view of her."

"What are you doing here?" Mark asked.

"Listening to my sister waste her talents with a load of losers like you."

"Your only talent is being an ass," he told Aaron.

Aaron laughed. "Better than being a wimp like you. You want to sucker punch someone again, you should aim for that guy." He pointed to the man Lily was talking to. "But even if you got rid of him, there will always be others after him. I know my sister. Lily's wild. She doesn't like to be pinned down. Especially to someone like you. She's not cut out for the boring junior executive type. She had her fling with you, and now it's over."

"I trust Lily completely," Mark said, truthfully. "We're happy together. Just because *you* don't know what faithfulness is . . ."

"Neither does my sister." Aaron pointed again to the man talking with Lily. "I bet she didn't tell you that guy was over the house yesterday."

What? Mark's heart started to race.

"And the day before that too. I saw them on the living room couch, as close as two people could be without having sex. And maybe they were about to have sex before I interrupted them. You should thank me for walking in on them."

"You bastard," Mark said.

"You pathetic loser," Aaron retorted. "Looks like Lily finally came to her senses and got sick of you and found someone else."

"I'm sure there's a good reason they're talking," Mark said. But he wasn't sure of anything right now. Was Lily seeing someone else? How could he have gone from feeling elated right after the show to feeling horrible now, just a few minutes later?

"If I were you, I'd watch my back." Aaron pounded him on the back, hard, before walking away.

Guyda approached him next. "Hey, I wasn't done talking to you. You kids were so great tonight, I want to get you into the spring music festival in Berkeley. You've heard of it, right?"

"Sure have!" Mark said.

"Yeah, it's really big. A lot of record producers go up there scouting for new talent. It could be Amber Road's big break."

"That would be great!" Mark said.

"You just have to make sure everyone can go," Guyda told him. "You'd drive up to Berkeley together, spend three nights and four days up there."

"We'll go," Mark said. "It'll be fantastic." *Lily will want to go on the road, be with me all the time, and play our songs.* He told himself that, anyway. He hoped she would. She was still talking to that man.

"I'm going to take off now," Guyda said. "Think about the music festival."

Mark nodded. "Thanks for everything. I'll definitely think about that a lot." He wasn't really thinking about the festival now though. He was thinking about Lily and love and longing, and he was anxious to put his thoughts and feelings down in words, set it to music, and create a new song for Amber Road.

Lily caught his eye and started walking toward him.

Mark said to himself once again, *I'm the luckiest guy in the world.*

Amber Road

beautiful girl

I fell in love today
Down at the beach by the
    waves
And our eyes met
And the sun set
The sky above us turning
    red and gold
Then he kissed me in the fading
    sun
He said I'm beautiful and
    I'm the one

I don't want to be the most
    beautiful girl
I just want to be the most
    beautiful girl for you
I don't want to be the only one
    in the world
I just want to be the only one
    for you

I fell in love today
Down at the beach in the sand
Don't ask me how
I just knew now
Nothing's gonna take our love
    away
Then he kissed me in the fading
    sun
He said I'm beautiful and
    I'm the one

I don't want to be the most
    beautiful girl
I just want to be the most
    beautiful girl for you
I don't want to be the only one
    in the world
I just want to be the only one
    for you

If it's right, right now
Why should I slow down
Don't let me touch the ground
Tonight!

I don't want to be the most
    beautiful girl
I just want to be the most
    beautiful girl for you
I don't want to be the only one
    in the world
I just want to be the only one
    for you

And now a special preview of the next
book in The Band series. . .

The Band
finding love

Coming from Berkley JAM
November 2007!!!

Lily Bouchet looked in her mirror to make sure she didn't have anything weird in her teeth, dabbed on some lipstick, grabbed her purse, and dashed out of her bedroom. It was Friday night and her boyfriend, Mark Carrelli, had just sent her a text message saying it was very important she meet him at the club a half hour earlier than usual.

She stopped in front of her twin brother Aaron's room and tapped on the door. They hadn't seen each other since school that day, but she was pretty sure he was in there with a girl. "Aaron, I'm going over to Waves," Lily said loudly. "I might not be home 'til late."

"Hold on a sec!" he shouted.

"I'm kind of in a hurry," Lily said.

He opened his bedroom door slightly, then came out and shut

the door behind him. He wore the red silk bathrobe their mother had bought him when she was filming in China last year.

"You off to the club?" he asked.

"Yeah," Lily said. "Have you seen or heard from Mom and Dad? Weren't they supposed to be back from Puerto Vallarta by now? I thought they were flying in this morning."

"Who can keep track of Mom and Dad and their travels?" Aaron said. "Who would even want to?"

Lily would. She really wished her parents would cut back on their travels. But Lily didn't tell Aaron that. "Do me a favor," she said. "When they come home, will you remind them that they promised to come listen to me at Waves tonight?"

"Sure. *If* they come home."

"What's that supposed to mean?" Lily asked.

Aaron shrugged. "It's just that they're not the most reliable people in the world. Actually, don't count on Dad at all. He got called to some meeting in Aspen, so he definitely won't be here. And Mom could be anywhere on the planet right now."

"Yeah," Lily admitted, "but she promised she'd come to Waves tonight. She's never heard me sing. Not in public, anyway." Lily wasn't sure her mom had ever heard her sing in private either. "I bet she'll like it."

"Anyone would like hearing you sing. You have a great voice. I just don't want you to get hurt, that's all," her brother said.

"Aaron?" the girl in his room called out.

"She's so demanding," Aaron told Lily with a grin.

Lily rolled her eyes. "I have to go meet Mark. Have fun."

"Mark." Her brother shook his head. "Feel free to break up with that loser boyfriend of yours."

"Knock it off," she told him.

"One day you'll come to your senses," Aaron said. "And you'll realize that your stupid boyfriend's stupid band is bringing you down. Your're better than Mark. Hell, Lily, you're better than everyone in your band combined."

"You're wrong. Amber Road is a great band," Lily said. "And the people in it are my friends."

"You are so deluded," he said. "Don't you know you have the talent to be out there on your own? If Joel Matthews makes you an offer to go solo, you'd better take it."

Joel Matthews was the music producer who showed up at the band's last gig, thanks to Aaron.

"Look," Lily said, "all Joel Matthews did was introduce himself and say he liked my singing. He didn't offer me a record contract or even an audition. So, while I appreciate you sending him that demo of me singing, I don't have any plans to ditch Amber Road."

"You'd be crazy not to," Aaron told her.

"I have to go." Lily rushed to the front door and out of the house.

Lily arrived at Waves at the same time as Sienna Douglas, the band's bass player. "Hey, Sienna, what are you doing here?" Lily asked, surprised to see her.

"I got a text message from Mark, telling me to come early," Sienna said. She nodded at the Volvo belonging to Tracie's mom, which was pulling up to the curb. "We all did, I guess."

"I wonder what's going on," Lily said.

"I would have thought you'd know," Sienna said.

If there was a barb in that, Lily ignored it. Things were still a little tense between her and Sienna. After all, Mark had dumped Sienna to go out with her. But ever since Sienna and Carter had fallen for each other, the tension between Sienna and her had eased.

Lily watched as Mrs. Grant, Tracie's mom, got out of the car and opened the trunk, taking out a set of crutches.

"I'll get her guitar, Mrs. G," Sienna offered, and grabbed Tracie's beloved Strat from the trunk.

"Need help?" Lily asked Tracie.

"No, I'm fine," Tracie said, taking one crutch from her mom and gingerly easing herself up and out of the car. Tracie had been on crutches since she got into a DUI accident the month before, banging herself up and destroying her parents' Beemer. Just yesterday, she'd exchanged her hard fiberglass cast for a walking cast.

"Man," Sienna exclaimed. "Look at you!"

"You look fantastic!" Lily agreed.

Tracie wore a peach rose in her blond hair, as she always did when they performed, but almost everything else about her hair was different. It was short and spiky now, and a lighter shade. It was almost platinum, like the color of white corn. She wore a soft, tight ivory sweater and a wrap skirt, and giant gold hoop earrings with a heavy gold necklace. She also had on more makeup than usual.

Tracie's mother stood in front of the passenger door of the Volvo, her arms crossed, one eyebrow raised.

"My mom thought I looked really sweet before," Tracie explained. "She thinks the new look—the new me—is trashy."

"I never said that," her mother objected.

"Not in so many words."

"You look hot," Lily said. "Like a blond gypsy. I don't think you look trashy at all."

Sienna seemed to bite back a grin, another thing Lily ignored. Lily was dressed in her usual style—a tight tank top with no bra, a miniskirt that barely covered her ass, and very high heels. Sienna had never actually said it to her face, but Lily would bet money that Sienna considered Lily's look total trash.

Sienna, on the other hand, joked that she was San Diego's only black preppie, and she looked it in her polo shirts and knee-length skirts.

Tracie waved good-bye to her mother and said, "Thanks a lot for the ride."

Tracie's mother remained standing in front of the car.

"We need to go into Waves," Tracie said.

"I want to see you perform tonight," her mother said.

Tracie winced. "You don't trust me."

"No, I don't, to be honest." Her mother frowned. "Not after all that's happened lately."

"Are you ever going to let me out of your sight?" Tracie asked.

"We'll keep an eye on her, Mrs. Grant. Don't worry." Sienna's voice sounded reassuring.

"Not that she needs keeping an eye on," Lily added. "She's really a good person."

"Thanks, but I think I'll look after her myself," Mrs. Grant said.

Tracie sighed. "Mom, this is a nightclub. Most of the music they play is rock—contemporary, not your seventies and eighties stuff. You're not going to hear any Neil Diamond or Duran Duran songs. Besides, you'd probably be the oldest person there."

"Not if I bring your father," her mother said.

"Please, Mom. No," Tracie begged.

Lily cleared her throat. "Well, my mom is coming tonight, and she's about your age, Mrs. Grant, even though she hates to admit it."

"Really? Your mother's coming?" Sienna asked.

Lily couldn't help smiling as she nodded. Finally, she would have a chance to show her mother the one thing she was good at, the one thing she really loved to do.

"Mom, feel free to go home and relax for the night," Tracie said.

"I will, and then I'll be back in time for your show," her mother promised as she got in the car.

"We should go," Lily said. "You know how Mark gets when anyone's five minutes late."

The three girls walked into the club together. The warm-up band—four Mesa College guys—was already playing. The girls waved at them as they walked behind the stage to the dressing room.

Mark was already there with George Yee, the band's drummer. Mark was scanning a song list and George was taking a set of drumsticks out of a zippered case.

Mark's gaze lit on Lily as they walked in. "Thanks for showing up early," he said, then pulled her into his arms for a hug.

Lily let herself relax against him for a moment. Being part of the band felt great. Being with Mark was the best thing that had ever happened to her.

"Whoa!" George pointed at Tracie. "Who is that fun-loving, crazy girl? And what has she done with sweet little Tracie?"

Tracie giggled.

"Hey, you get a haircut or something?" Mark said, releasing Lily.

"Mark!" Lily rolled her eyes. "Tracie's got an entire new look, and you ask if she got a haircut or something."

Mark shrugged. "At least I noticed. You look good, Trace."

"Thanks," Tracie said. "So why did you have us come early?"

"I have some news . . . some pretty incredible news."

"So spill," Sienna urged him.

"Okay. Our excellent manager, Steve Guyda, told me something really exciting."

"Which is—?" Lily asked.

Mark smiled. "Have you heard of the Berkeley Blowout going on next week?"

"Of course," George said. "It's the new music fest everyone's talking about. The hottest bands are all supposed to be there. I want to drive up and check them out if I can scrounge together enough money for the admission and gas."

"Oh, right," Lily said. "I just saw something about it on the Net. It's supposed to be amazing."

"Well, Guyda's been bugging the organizers to let us play there," Mark said.

"Us? Play there?" George sounded as if he were in shock.

"Yes, 'us play there,'" Mark said. "It's during our Spring Break, so it's perfect timing."

Lily couldn't believe it either. "Did Guyda actually say they'll let us play?"

"No. Not yet. But there's a scout from the festival coming to hear us perform."

"When?" Sienna asked.

"Tonight," Mark said.

"Tonight? Wow." Lily clapped her hand over her mouth. *This was it. The band's chance to break out.*

"This is so cool!" George's eyes were bulging. "Going up to Berkeley with you guys would be a blast. And then performing there would be, I don't know . . . incredible!"

Tracie looked even paler than usual. "Really?" she murmured in a small voice. "I think I'm getting bad stage fright."

"Relax," Mark said. "We know these songs and we know how to play 'em. All we have to do is go out there tonight and kick it. We're gonna rock the house."

"But I still have this cast on," Tracie said. "I look like such a nerd in it. I don't want to ruin things for you guys."

"That's why I didn't mention the scout being here before tonight," Mark said. "I didn't want you to get all crazy-worried."

"Tracie, you look really good." Lily touched her arm.

"No one's even going to notice your cast," Sienna said. "Besides, people are here because of our music, not our legs."

"That's what they say, but I know they're really here for my legs," George said, extending one slightly chubby jeans-clad leg. "They're irresistible."

Tracie laughed. "Sorry to act all paranoid. I'm just a little nervous."

"If you really want to be nervous, think about what the Berkeley Blowout could mean," Mark said. "It could be a major move forward for Amber Road. It's good P. R., for one thing. And we would be on the same bill as some excellent bands. Maybe they'll think of us if they need an opening act. Plus, there should be all sorts of people from the music industry—radio station managers, reporters, maybe even record producers."

"Well, that really helped calm me down. Not," Tracie said.

Or me, Lily thought. The idea of her mom finally showing up at one of her performances already made her nervous. Now everything seemed to be on the line. They had to be brilliant tonight. Absolutely, totally brilliant.

"We'll all burn up the stage," Mark promised. "Let's get out there. We have a talent scout to impress."

"Right." Lily took a deep breath and headed toward the stage.

As Lily sang the lead on Amber Road's newest song, "Tomorrow," she studied the audience. Waves was packed tonight. And it wasn't just the weekend night that made the club crowded. Amber Road was building an audience. Every day they were getting more friends and downloads from MySpace, more hits on their website, and more e-mails from fans. A lot of the people in the audience had heard them before and returned for more.

When Lily joined Amber Road less than a year ago, she never imagined that as high school seniors, they would be headlining at one of the best clubs in San Diego. After tonight's show, they could very well be invited to perform at the Berkeley Blowout. *Smile,* Lily told herself. *You've got it made.*

But as she searched the crowd and couldn't find what she was looking for, her smile became harder and harder to maintain.

She tried. The other band members were playing so well tonight, she didn't want to disappoint them. Despite her bad leg, Tracie had ignored the chair put onstage for her, and instead stood next to Sienna. She and Sienna were perfect tonight—Tracie ripping through her guitar solos with full-on passion and Sienna playing the bass like she owned every note. Mark showed that the keyboard was high art and sang with controlled intensity. And George was crazy on drums, as if he was having the best time of his life. *Her probably is,* Lily thought, *while I'm just trying not to fall apart onstage.*

She told herself to appreciate what she had, and not to wish for what she didn't have. She had a wonderful boyfriend and a role as lead singer in a band she loved.

Next to her, Mark crooned, "Tomorrow I'll wake up next to you, gazing at your sunshine face, your silky curves, your giving lips." He had written the song for her. He reached out and stroked her cheek as he sang.

She willed tears not to fall on his hand, and smiled, smiled,

smiled as she searched the audience. She still couldn't find her mother. As much as Lily told herself to be happy, she just couldn't tonight.

She came in for their final duet. "Today next to you, tomorrow next to you, always my love next to you." She felt Mark looking into her eyes, but she couldn't meet his gaze. She needed to search the crowd one more time. Her mother had *promised* to show up. Lily had not only talked to her about it two weeks ago, she'd put *Lily performs at Waves, 9:00* on the wall calendar with a red pen. Yesterday, she'd even sent her parents an e-mail reminder and a text message.

But she hadn't come, after all. Lily had thought this time would be different. This time her mother would be there. This time her mother would show her that she loved her.

"Tomorrow," Lily sang to close the song. But tomorrow wouldn't be any different for her. Her mother would still be a lot more interested in her travels and parties and acting gigs than in her daughter.

The crowd applauded wildly. Lily nodded to them, all the while thinking, *I don't deserve this. I was far from my best tonight. Besides, I'm not any good. If I was, my mother would have been here. She likes whatever's hot and buzz-worthy, and I guess I'm neither. The audience is just being nice.*

She peered at them once again, recognizing a lot of faces from school and from other shows, but not the one face she really wanted to see.

Then Lily felt her stomach go into free fall as she saw another face, a familiar face.

What was *he* doing here?